T5-CQF-300

3 2109 00 28 5682

Comic Novel

Douglas H. Young

1987
NEW DIRECTIONS PUBLISHING HOUSE
Chicago • New York

Library of Congress Catalog Card Number 85-63470

ISBN 0-9606510-1-2

FIRST EDITION

TO
Barbara

ALSO BY DOUGLAS YOUNG

The Tidy Bowl Man Lives
and
Jiffy John
(Two Comic Novellas)

Non Fiction

How Peace Came To The World
(Co-contributor)

$$HT = HT$$

1

HORACE SANK INTO his armchair with a beer and the evening paper. Had that been a shout? Maybe from the apartment next door, Christmas carollers—perhaps his mother-in-law demanding something from the bathroom. Blasted woman always visited at the wrong time. That could translate to mean any time, couldn't it? The room seemed to tremble slightly—another tremor? Now Ethel's voice above the howl of the Pross-All blender.

"...that mother, Horace? Find out...hands full..."

Horace. Why didn't she have a nickname for him?: Champ or even Buster. *Horace, Horace Stickle.* The initials lewd, the name a canker that always stung, an identification tag which relegated him to the category of odd and that somehow placed the stamp of loser on his brow. Pumping for leverage, he made it to his feet, dizzy, wobbling. Middle-aged and balding, overweight for a shorty. Could the barometer of his health be falling, storms moving in? What had the doctor said last time?: something about blood pressure?: silent killers, the body's Mafia with contracts out. Maybe he'd explode and zip round the room like a deflating balloon, splutter out a window. No chance yet to tell Ethel the gossip Priddle had relayed: the hint of a promotion at Company that might redeem him from finishing his career in the twilight zone, raise him to lance corporal from private, color him something except grey.

"Mother Granger, can I get you something?"

"I can't hear you, Horace. Blender, I'm blending the health food."

"I was...to your mother, dear! Would you turn off?..."

But she couldn't hear. Never heard much of anything he'd had to say over the last few years. Too busy with women's rights, karate, and night courses in things he hadn't paid much attention to. Maybe if he'd shown more interest, the situation would be different. Hard to know.

"Mother Granger, could I? ...is there anything?..." Silence. Was she in one of her difficult *not speaking* moods? Fallen asleep in the bath?

"Horace, tell mother dinner's almost ready. Her rutabaga salad is on the table, jellied consommé too. Does she need?—"

"MOTHER GRANGER, ETHEL SAYS YOUR SALAD AND SOUP—"

"Horace, for heaven's sake, do you have to yell? She isn't deaf. No wonder she won't answer, shouting at her. Let me...She doesn't like anyone talking to her in there. You know she's sensitive about that."

"Then why did you ask me to?...Forget it."

Not deaf, alright—could hear a pin drop in outer space, but nothing he ever had to say. Tuned him out unless he was due for a lecture on what she saw as his failure: that he wasn't a real man, a role she seemed to feel only women could fill.

He could see her now, a spindly shrub in a storm, the arms sawing and whirling, hands and fingers chopping, spearing, looping a semaphore of disapproval. Then she would seal the indictment, convict, be judge and jury, pronounce the sentence: useless like most men, especially her favorite target, Randolf, the husband who'd gambled away his money and died shortly afterwards. Undaunted, nevertheless, Mums, according to Ethel, had a *gentleman friend*.

"Mother dear, dinner's ready. Can I get you a towel, anything? Horace didn't mean to be rude. He doesn't realize how loud his voice is."

2

"See, she won't even talk to you. I told you…"

"*Moth*—er. *Din*—ner. Horace apologizes for shouting. Apologize Horace."

"Yes, Mum…sorry about that, Mother Granger. Didn't mean to upset you."

Ethel loomed over him in her platform heels, those abominable shoes that emphasized her height, made him feel like a monkey on a chain as he hurried after her on the street, while she sailed on ahead, a giant kite that filled his horizon.

Once she'd worn slippers or flats, been willowy and slender with eyes that danced and sparkled an impish blue. That was in the beginning, though. Gradually over the last few years the softness and gaiety had disappeared; the curves becoming angular; height imposing, gangling; the muscles ropy and hard; eyes cold and almost accusing. At times she seemed to rise before him like a powerful electrical transformer dwarfing and smothering him, a force bent on short circuiting his system, blowing his fuses, indeed perhaps erasing his existence.

Couldn't Ethel go her way, he his, without the competitive fury? Then again, how did he appear to her? Hadn't she called him a "wimp" or "quiche-eater" during a recent argument, overheard Mum Granger about the same time confide to Ethel he was a "bland pudding of a man, sort of *mousey?*"

"I don't understand, Horace. There isn't a sound. You've probably insulted her. MOTHER, WILL YOU PLEASE ANSWER ME? HORACE IS GONE. Go away, she probably wants to talk privately. I said go…"

"Fine, maybe I'll go out for dinner. *Rutabaga, jellied whatever.* Enough to turn one's stomach. She ought to give up chocolates—boxes everywhere. Mum's an addict, you know, chocoholic."

"Ridiculous. She loves health food, Horace: brewers yeast, sprouts. They're alive with vitamins and minerals. Something that might give you what it takes. We'll discuss it later. Now will you?…What?…Did you hear that?…"

"Sounded like a bit of a splash—"

"Nothing of the kind, something sliding."

"Hah, fallen asleep, no doubt."

"Ridiculous, she takes cold baths."

"Maybe forty winks on the toilet then. She hogs that for

3

hours. Prunes, why not prunes instead of all that health gunk? That's what she..."

"You won't talk that way in front of her. I won't have it. Do you hear me? Do I make myself clear, Horace? Now Mother, this isn't like you, I must come in."

"How, my dear? No doubt the door is double-locked."

"Your fault, Horace—walking in on her that time. It was terribly upsetting. Now stand back. *Hah, hut!"*

"Lord, how'd you do that? You've broken...The whole panel's caved in."

"Can break a brick in half too. My instructor, Rolf, has a superior Black Belt. Wood is child's play. Move away, will you please. We don't want her scared again. I'll just reach in and turn the handle..."

"*Scared*? What do you think that crash will?..."

"Mother, are you?...Good grief! Don't come in, Horace. Get out of here! Have you no decency? Get an ambulance immediately. Did you hear me? Move."

"Artificial respiration, that PR thing, try!..."

But of course Ethel was already doing that: blowing, thumping, squeezing. Someday he might be under those hands too, lethal clubs that would split him in half easy as a rotten pumpkin. How did one get an ambulance, the police? Wasn't there a special number?

"Horace, dial nine, eleven."

"Yes, I know, I'm doing it. I have it."

Why had he been about to dial operator? An ambulance wasn't really needed, though. The blue face and spaghettied tangle of limbs in the tub told the story. Whatever emergency there had been was over. Mother Granger for certain had gone wherever she was going after life on earth. The hands forever stilled, the symphony on the fate of men, himself, over for good. Or was it? Would Ethel carry on, redouble?...

"Hello, this is an emergency. An ambulance, we need an ambulance. My mother-in-law is in the bathtub. Address?...I ...The Battle Ax, I mean Arms, Apartments. I'm sure she's dead, but— It's 1661, no 1166 Rostow Avenue. Just a minute."

Damn pounding at the door. Why couldn't people knock? Probably Widow Gribbley bashing away with her walker to complain about noise or many of the other problems she

4

seemed to trace his way. "Yes, I'm here, coming, a minute please!"

He was a sliver of a man in black, the fedora shadowing a chalky face that knifed towards him.

"Police. There's been a complaint: screaming allegedly issuing from this dwelling."

"Yes, come in. It's my mother-in-law in the bathroom. Dead, I'm sure she is, but...That way, down there. Excuse, I'm on the phone...an ambulance..."

"Hello, Stickle speaking. What? No, I didn't kill...Apartment Eleven D. Thank you."

"I'm Detective Karaki. Did I hear you say *kill*? Your mother-in-law—did you kill her?"

"No no, of course..."

"I'm recording everything, sir. It's all going down on tape. Anything you say—"

"Have you phoned, Horace? Was that the door?"

"Who is that? You said *of course*. You *did* kill?—"

"No I didn't kill...My wife, it's my wife."

"Your *wife* is the one, *she* killed?..."

"This way, Detective Karaki, down the hall. I'll explain. She must have slipped..."

"Who is this man, Horace? We need an ambulance, a doctor, immediately. It may be too late. What is the matter with you!"

"You, your name ma'am?"

"No time for questions. Can't you see?...busy..."

"It's my mother-in-law, Detective—"

"Are you his mother-in-law, ma'm?"

"Rubbish. Both of you, out of here. I can handle this."

"Yes ma'm, I'm afraid though there'll have to be some questions. We like to clear up our homicides. We have modern technology, the latest in detection equipment. We usually get to the bottom...Ah, those chocolates on the basin. Excuse, must check everything, everyone, out. Not to worry, sir: If you're innocent, we'll know, find out. Mothers, mothers-in-law, wives, dads—a round-robin of mayhem and murder, if there ever was. All in the family. Mmmmm, yes indeed. Love breeds hate, hate festers, erupts in violence, killing, massacre. Bloodlines decimated, relatives eliminated, children...Majored

5

in abnormal psychology, philosophy; I know, oh yes, there are things...Phishhh, the hair oil bottle on the tub. Seems to have spilled. Slippery, slippery. Is it yours, Mr.?...Did you put it there?—intentionally?"

"Yes it's mine, but I left it in the cabinet. She must have taken it out and—"

"Both of you—I won't say it again—out! She's gone. It's over. Do you understand? *Do you?* I want a moment alone."

"Of course, to be sure, my apologies. Got carried away. The phone, Mr. Stickle, I must use it. There are things to be done, many loose ends."

"In the other room, it's there, the phone. The door, someone knocking. Use the phone. Yes—oh, Mrs. Gribbley. What?..."

"Screamin', fightin'—sounded sumpin terrible. Weasley said a cop car was out front. Came quick this time. My Fred, he never ever made with the noise at me. Never till his dyin' day. He was a good man, Stickle, all man. Do you know what I mean? Do you? Why I'll bet you can't even—"

"Mrs. Gribbley, please, not so loud. People will think there's trouble. There is, but..."

Doors were already opening though. Heads popping in and out. Damn Mrs. Gribbley. Deaf. Had to yell to hear herself think. Loud enough to raise the dead (well, hopefully not Mums). Terrible way to think. Nothing funny about death. On his mind a lot lately. What was it like? Painful? An afterlife?: Heaven and Hell, a duplex with passes upstairs and down; the sighting of old friends, acquaintances? Reunion with Mums?—not so good. Maybe the women went somewhere else: a *His* and *Hers* restrooms sort of thing. Perhaps...

"Oh Jesus what!..." Pain, a silver flash, then digging, drilling at his foot. "Mrs. Gribbley, get your bloody walker *off* ..." Only a scowl as she careened away muttering, ramming doors, anything in her way.

Two faces popping around the door of the next apartment. Not the Dranes. They must have moved—died? A siren's wailing closer closer, then winding down, a final squawk.

Dizzy, shaky, leaning back against the wall. Now many faces, rising moons, all clenched and inching forward in the hall. The men in white brush quickly past while someone clutches at his sleeve. So soon they're back and gone on

6

rubbered feet, a tiny shape beneath the stretcher blanket pulled full length.

Karaki's face, a bony blade, was slicing words he barely heard except the final ones concerning "something more than meets the eye, but facts will out." And finally Ethel sweeping past to leave without a word.

At last alone, fatigued and drained. No doubt a thorough physical was long overdue, food too. But he wasn't hungry. What had Karaki meant about the hair oil?—"slippery slippery." Did accusation somehow slither through the words?

He didn't recall turning on the TV. Why was the bald man laughing hysterically, slapping his thighs, drumming his shoes furiously on the floor? He'd never know because the sound was off, and now the picture too. A brand new set. Perhaps the tremors, a faulty tube, a broken heart. *All gone, sir; she's dead, insides shot.*

Was he talking to himself again? Head buzzing—a fizzing tingle at the skull. Cork loose, the opener's tug more insistent these days. Dark now. Lights gone. Brownout, breakdown— everywhere, all over the world, maybe the universe. Inside Horace Stickle? No, his bulb was still lit, for now, anyway.

Moonlight touched the table catching the jellied consommé in a quivering silver. The slight form under the blanket, though, had been so still—for Mums. Strange, he thought, heading for the bedroom, so hard to figure out what you felt at times, and if you did, no one seemed to understnad your explanations anyway. But Ethel would understand *promotion*. And there was a chance that reward was moving in his direction, a rising elevator long overdue.

2

"DID YOU HEAR me, Horace?"

"The *blender*, turn it down. What?"

"Mother's urn, you will be picking it up, of course?"

"Yes Ethel. Where is she, I mean the urn?"

Feeling lightheaded again, dizzy, and it was only breakfast. Ethel's face, tiny, distant, a pea on a far horizon. Had to have a checkup. Probly not eating properly. Look at his egg: fried, not sunnyside up, a pancake congealed to a slimy mess. Why couldn't *she* cook it, be a housewife, stop whirling her metabolic boosters in the Pross-All: porridgy gunk that smelled...

"At Katzenbach's, Katzenbach's Parlor. Here, I've written it down. Something important is happening today, Horace. Took place almost overnight. Meant to tell you. But with Mums and everything...All work out for the best, though. Have to run, may be late."

"Could be I'll have a bit of news tonight too that..."

Wham. The door seemed to vibrate. Perhaps one day she would split it in half. Hard to believe she'd changed so much over the last few years. Feminism—was that it? Why couldn't they be feminist and feminine? Maybe the "vulnerable" man had forced the move, left a macho vacuum. Could that explain the return of hulks to the screen, men who even seemed to flex their faces, sport muscled eyes. Probly the wrong questions. No wonder he didn't understand the answers. "Stone age thinking, Horace, dinosaur mentality." Hadn't that been her response to his ideas on the subject?

Getting ahead was a virtue Ethel'd stressed frequently over the last year or two. Perhaps she'd been referring to herself: planning a move from the general typing pool at Corrugated to a secretary's position. Likely, though, the comment was directed at him—a hint, threat: start passing cars, speed up, or he'd be taken off the road and fined, lose his license, end up in jail. Ridiculous, imaginary shadows; but growing longer, darker, these days.

Well, Priddle had said the big meeting would be today. The tortoise usually won the race. It had taken a long time, but justice usually prevailed. He'd accept his prize with humility and there'd be a new chapter in his life to read. Ethel would be delighted, things would change.

Was the door still vibrating? Perhaps the tremors. Too late to pick up the urn before work. Far away the whine of sirens: police, ambulances—white men in rubber shoes. Would he go out like Mum Granger?: a shapeless mass under a tarp or towel. Something else to ponder. Later though. Amalgamated called. A siren of another kind. And that was one to heed, wasn't it. He'd pick the urn up at lunch hour. No rush. Mum Granger could wait, even if Amalgamated Foods wouldn't— not for him, anyway.

The park bench was cold. He was cold. The little package in his hands felt cold. He held it up to his ear, and shook the urn. Something clattered. Impossible, only ashes, human ashes. Maybe Mum's were of a different texture, spiritual noisemakers.

"'TIS THE SEASON TO BE MERRY. FA LA LA LA LA, LA LA LA *LA*. GIVE BREWBUSTER AND WIN A FRIEND." The truck was a squat bottle with speakers blaring. Yule had arrived, like it or not.

Had the urn actually rattled? Try again. Yes, there was

definitely...

"Cocktail shaker, my good man? Strange, the shape, I mean. Myself, the liver's shot, heart ruined. Two months, the doctors say—"

"Pardon? —No, It's not...nothing to drink. Mother Granger, she's...An urn, I just got it, them—ashes..."

The man, a bundle of rags reeking of zoos and barnyards. A cork protruding from the paper bag in his lap.

"A mother...Yes, church. Maybe He could help, understand. My friend, I have sinned, committed adultery, fornicated with creatures that—"

"You don't understand, not a nun, my mother-in-law. She died, killed herself, in the bathtub, slipped. It wasn't—"

"Death is upon us all, my son. He died that you might live. My wife, she drowned at Kruger's Baths." Eyes, cherries twirling, breath a high proof mist. "A great lady. Naked, in the waters. Two months, I've got...to celebrate. A toast, here—"

"No, I really..."

Now what? A huge black woman jostling, bumping against him to make way for herself and a large shopping bag. The old man offering him a bottle of dark liquid. Why not, why the hell not? A wake for Mum. A pill to dull the pain if the afternoon meeting went badly. Anything to kill the raw wind that knifed through him, swirled around the garbage pail lifting bits of newspaper and refuse into the air, hurling it into the street, around his legs. "Yes yes, perhaps just one little..." The urn, had to be careful..."Lady, would you mind?...this package...hold..."

"Aint no dope, is it? Man's like you sucking up juice middle the day, oughta be 'shamed. Takin' the welfare, ahness people's money. Gives it here. Mah man duh same way. No good. 'Roan,' I sez, 'you aint worth honky spit.'"

"Thank you. Careful please, very breakable."

The drink was strong, odor of disinfectant. One was plenty— well, why not two, and a dividend for the road before...

A shadow, footsteps, gleaming brogues, brass buttons and then the badge. A cratered face with visored brow. Overhead and pressing down, the sky, a silver grey of burning cold that teared his eyes and made him blink. Words spiked air, frozen bullets in his ear. "Be taking your name; complaints against

11

this sort of thing lately."

And his own voice, hoarse, cracking, answering "Amalgamated Foods" to some question, his name to another. The black woman moving to the end of the bench. The old man rising, muttering it wasn't *his* bottle, scurrying away. The policeman handing him a slip of paper, tossing the wine in the trash bin. Then to his feet and into traffic. "Fa La La La La La La La La," roared the Brewbuster truck on a return sweep, almost running him over as he weaved across the street to the subway.

"Ho Ho Ho," chanted the Santa inside the station. "Ho Ho Ho. *Mare*ree Christmas."

Oh that it would be, he hoped, the faint rumble indicating his train was on the way.

"Ladies and gentlemen, I've called this meeting of managers and assistant managers and other senior personnel to make a few brief announcements. First, Earl Battle, the *late* Mr. Earl Battle, your prior Vice-President, Personnel, was killed while on vacation last week at Alpine Heaven. An accident on the slopes. Ski pole in the brain. Quick, painless. No problems. He didn't suffer.

"My name is Harriet Mawsley, *Miz* Harriet Mawsley. Before that—and I see no reason to fudge the matter—I was Henry Mawsley. I am the new V.P. Seated beside me is Miz Ethel Trench who will fill the recently created position of Assistant V.P. of Personnel. Both of us have had extensive experience at Corrugated. Before that I was a union organizer with Bellow Steel. Now..."

"Stickle, did you hear?...Jesus, are you asleep? Those... that ...they're going to be running...It's..."

"What?...Damn it all, Priddle, not sleeping. Tired..."

"You're drunk, Stickle, I can smell it. You'd better listen. I'd advise—"

"Fine, Priddle, whatever..."

The man had a Humpty Dumpty head, a gleaming missile zeroing in. It was almost impossible to hear or see. Smoke filled the tiny room and his ears felt clogged. As a Group

Four, he wasn't entitled to sit at the table, but was jammed against the wall in a wooden chair with many others. Still, if nothing else, he was senior personnel, twenty five years of senior. Stickle Senior, with no son, no promotion in years. Only rotation through the other sections. Horizontal, not vertical trajectory. No moon shots for him, not yet anyway. What had the gigantic woman said?: She was Henry? Hard to see through the haze. Eyes streaming, burning, the wine fuming in his nose. The other woman—must be a coincidental resembl...Was it *Ethel?* A pinstriped pantsuit, charcoal-gray, black ascot. Hair a darkling slash across her brow. Squint you fool, rub your eyes. It's a dream. He'd wake up, be back on the park bench clutching Mum Granger. Everything would be okay, not...

"...In short, ladies and gentlemen, things need to be reviewed, revised, some functions added, others eliminated. Snatly and Broadspringer, top management consultants, will be looking at the whole headquarters' organization of Amalgamated."

"Hah, maybe you're about to be deleted, Stickle."

"Priddle, goddam, stop whispering, I can't hear what..."

Had the woman been looking at him when she said *eliminated?* The size of an All Pro tackle, she dwarfed the conference table. His eyes cleared momentarily. Yes, it *was*...

"She's a man, Stickle, Harriet's a man. Look at the five o'clock shadow. I tell you..."

"Priddle, for Christ's sake, my wife, it's...!"

"Your wife, is it now, Stickle? Lovely. Did you drink the whole bottle?"

"Shut up, she's looking, pointing, our way..."

"Do the two gentlemen over there have anything to add? I see, *nothing.* Well, to continue..."

Good Lord it *was* Ethel. The other creature's finger—large enough to indict a congregation—had rifled out sighting him or Priddle or both of them. Ethel stared at him, her legs crossed, one foot circling slowly, the platform shoe taking aim.

Miz Trench: using her maiden name. Going back to her roots, her pre-Stickle condition. Like Mum after Dad died.

"...And these two gentlemen, Mr. Ripstrom Futts and Mr. Robert Joblobber, have been assigned by the Snatly and Broadspringer management firm to Personnel. I am sure you

13

will make every effort to cooperate..."

"Psst, Stickle, yonder the executioners, eh?"

"I've seen them somewhere..."

"Maybe they're Henry's brothers, Roberta and—"

"No, their faces are familiar, I just can't place..."

They seemed to be eying him, taking his measure, fuel or fodder? Now nodding at each other, verdict unanimous. Where? ...yes, the walker, Mrs. Gribbley's walker on his toe that night, two heads poking around the corner of a door. Them, it was those two alright. "The night Mum Granger slipped, killed...I...They're in my building, Priddle, live on the same floor..."

"Off your nut, Stickle. They saw you *kill* your mum? Better sober..."

"...and so a word from Messrs. Futts and Joblobber. Mr. Futts."

"Greeting. Tempus fugit. So may some of you. Briefly our job is to attack fat, excise it on sight, automate it out of existence at headquarters. As the military decree: We want you to become a lean, mean, fighting machine. Microchips, silicon, electronics, communications, computers—high-tech is the wave of the future. You'll either be on it or deep-sixed. We want Company—*you*—on a starvation diet, every calorie burned: $E=mc^2$. A lump of coal could light New York for a year. We want Personnel lit the same way: little mass, lots of light. That's it. No more, no less."

Futts had definitely been eying him when he finished. What did he mean— *little mass?:* condensed information, fewer bodies?

Strange looking man: bald, small, almost dwarfish. The nose, hooked, a beak: An owl at midnight hovering low, its talons flexed, the yellowed eye in ceaseless search: sky-shark forever closing in. Beware mice, take care, Horace. You may feed his appetite, join Mum....

"...And now, Mr. Joblobber."

No owl, this one. A robin redbreast, cocker spaniel snuggling up.

"What, Stickle, another friend? An *owl* you say?"

Had he spoken? Better watch himself. Was the room tilting slightly, spinning a bit? Joblobber, seemed to rise in sections,

14

so tall, elegant, hair a ripple of grey. At least he looked friendly. Smiling, raisin eyes twinkling in a florid face, he was the incarnation of business success. Why couldn't *he* look like that?: gold watch chain looped over the vest, a commander in charge. Ah, now the pipe, stuffed, deliberately tamped, contents lit, sucked upon, then blown gravely into life: little cloud-puffs, smoke words, that spun silently toward him, the incense of a power and knowledge he would never have, a semaphore of peace and good tidings. Robert Joblobber would understand, be a soul brother, one of *us* rather than *them*. About to speak, beaming at everyone, *him*, a final drawing at the pipe.

"Ladies and gentlemen, let me say just one thing. I agree entirely with Ripstrom, Mr. Futts. It will all be done with your best interests in mind; your past, present and whatever future you, ah...um, can anticipate with this wonderful worldwide conglomerate. Thank you."

"He just sat on your future, Stickle. Heh heh."

"Look Priddle!..."

The man was a rash that flared everywhere given half a chance. Yet it was true: promotion, prospects, always seemed a mirage that became reality for someone else. Could he ever have been the kid who daydreamed—believed?—of being a hero, the conqueror in white astride his battlements, throngs blackening the horizon, chanting his name, as he reached out his arms roaring?: *"And I say unto you..."*

"I want to see you in my office, Mr. Stickle—now."

"Pardon?...*Ethel*, who do you think?...You can't tell me..."

But she *had* told him and swept past, her legs pinstriped scissors scything rapidly ahead, a thin leather briefcase tucked under one arm. In the black platform heels, she even topped Priddle eeling at her side, hands sculpting airy points to attract her attention

Ripstrom scuttled past with a quick stare, while Joblobber cleared the door in streamers of smoke. Was he humming?

Far ahead, Ethel strode down the hall towards old Battle's domain, then wheeled out of sight. Earl, to coin a silly phrase, had lost the battle alright, but not the war. He'd left that to others. The problem was who was on what side and what was at stake? Was there even a war? He'd better try to find out, and damned fast.

15

*

"Look here Ethel, what?—"

"*Miz Trench*, Mister Stickle, Miz Trench. I had the decency not to embarrass you with your surname. You will reciprocate. Sit down."

"I have no intention—"

"In that chair, Mr. Stickle, and please close the door."

"I *will* not..."

Dizzy, was he going to faint? Must be something more than the wine. The chair, so low; felt as if he were sitting on the floor. Light poured through the windows, blinding, dazzling white. Where was Ethel? That dark silhouette behind the desk, voice remote, clipped? Words zinging past, bouncing off walls, each other, his head—bursting bubbles disappearing into the sun's fluorescence: "Masters degree...computer technology...moved up...wouldn't listen...secretary, then assistant to Henry...Harriet...doctorate in a year..."

"Hor...Mister Stickle, have you been listening? We'll talk later. Meetings, many things to do, *important* things. I..."

"Harriet, come in. Is there something?..."

"Schoner, Rathbone Schoner. General Attorney. Ten minutes, his office. Problem here?"

"No, this is Mr. Stickle, Personnel Research, Group Four."

"Hmm, the face. Yes, from the meeting. Thought you had something to say. We must keep *shush* though, mustn't we, if we don't want to contribute. Indeed we must. In ten then, dearie. Ciao."

"Goddamn it..."

"You will not swear in this office, Mr. Stickle, or proper disciplinary measures will be taken. Believe me, home is home, office is office. A different can of worms, to use the vernacular. You picked up the urn, didn't you?"

"Yes, *Miz Trench,* I picked up that can of—"

"Fine, you can go—for now."

"Ciao, *dearie.*"

Sweat beading his forehead, soaking his shirt. Was she shouting? *Discipline*?: cold baths, electric prods, the iron maiden? Whack his hands with a ruler, unhinge them with a karate chop?

"Getting your oar in already, eh, Stickle. Better row harder, boat's leaking, sharks circling. Davy Jones awaits, Stickle. Ciao."

"Look here, Priddle, I resent..."

Out of earshot already. Always wrong. The man forever got things snarled, the information garbled. Maybe it was deliberate, his idea of a practical joke. *A biggie meeting, promotions.*

Mums wouldn't have the last laugh on this one, though — daughter in the catbird seat. No, not this time. Mums was elsewhere and she...She — Jesus, *she* was sitting on top of the black woman's shopping bag. Hurry, if he ran back — , no, a cab...Joblobber and Futts coming towards him.

"Enjoy, Mr. Stickle, enjoy."

"Thank you, Mr. Joblobber, same to —"

"She was dead, was she not, Stickle?"

"Yes, Mr. Futts, it's her urn. I must —"

"No time to lose, Stickle, is there? It's money in the bank, a new currency. *Time.*"

"Yes..."

Gone in clouds of smoke. They knew his name. Must've checked his mailbox. Perhaps Mum was still there, in the bag on the bench. Futts was right; time was valuable. Mums had none left. With luck, though, some still remained in his account.

3

WOULD THE COLORED woman still be there? It'd been over an hour. Maybe she'd figure he'd be back, reward her for keeping the parcel. Yes, she just might...Was that the lady? He tapped a shoulder and was immediately doubled over by a backhand to the stomach. On her feet, whirling, a mountain of coal towering above him, pink combs bristling from under a bonnet.

"I...Mum...the package was..." Hard to breathe, eyes streaming. "She...it..."

"I'se aint your mama, bimbo. Nobody cops a feel off Flossie, you jive turkey. Youse want *pohlice,* I'll..."

"There it is, on top...your shopping bag. Let me...Don't you recognize?..."

"No way, Hambone. Ain't never seen you. Touchin', feelin', grabbin'..."

"Lady, Flossie..."

"Only the Roan call me Flossie. I Mrs. Vanders to you. Now get outta mah face fore I makes trouble."

"Mrs. Vanders, I must have the parcel. It's an urn, my mother-in-law, Mum Granger. She's in there. Please..."

Hopeless, the woman had been drinking, eyes a film of red, breath winey.

"Mum in dere, eh? Maybe duh Roan too with the genie? Rub it, they both flies out on the rug? Hah. I'se off now, Whitey. Ciao."

"No!..."

He lunged around the bench and grabbed the package with both hands. Out of the corner of his eye he saw the buckled shoe coming and jumped sideways. The shopping bag whistled over his head. Her great fingers pried and wrenched at the package. The woman was yelling. Now the other shoe smashed into his shin. He fell onto the bench and scrambled to one end. People were gathering. She was reaching for him again. Somehow he was on his feet staggering towards a cab, then inside. A crash, window starring from a savage blow, the cab squealing into traffic.

"Almost gottcha, didn't she, Sammy? Saw youse lift her parcel. Me, I mind my own business. Always can use a little extra, though—know what I mean?..."

"*Steal?* It's *my* package. She kicked...The box here...my wife's—Mum, I mean, she's in it...her ashes...I..."

"*What?* Yuh fried your old lady? Look mister, I don't want nothin'..." He pulled to the curb and flipped open a back door. "Out. Stealin's one thing, murder..."

"You don't understand..."

Back on the street. A truck showered him with slush and snow squalls stung his eyes. A bell was ringing nearby. The angular face loomed redly above him, arms sawing and waving. A uniform, brass buttons, visored hat, pressed close. He stumbled backwards against a bubble filled with money.

"Give something, anything...help," came the voice now directly above him, hoarse, demanding. "We need more, whatever you can..."

The bell jangled beside his ear, on and on and...The person—was it female?—fingered a tiny calculator.

"More to go over the top, please..."

Coins fell from his hand to the pavement.

"FA LA LA LA LA..."

Brewbuster on a different tack. He lurched away into a blast of wind. Cold, God he was freezing, numb. Shaking, he pushed

20

through revolving doors and was swept up in a wave of shoppers. But it was warm, that was the important thing. Flow with the crowd, the torrent of babble that raged over him.

Somebody jolted him from behind. He lost his balance and fell to one side grabbing for support. Something ripped and a body fell into his arms. Creamy buttocks brushed against his nose. Blond hair hung to one side over a gleaming skull. Whirlpools of laughter sucked at him. The crowd pressed closer, jamming the thing up over his head. A breast brushed his mouth. He couldn't see anything. Suddenly he was in a chair with the mannequin draped across his lap, pink underwear in his fist. The thing was bald, one leg bent backwards at a crazy angle. Someone was talking to him, had tapped his shoulder.

Looking up he saw a small, balding man with a hairline mustache that wiggled upwards, a caterpillar smiling. The underwear was eased from his hand, and the mannequin lifted. A badge on the man's jacket read "Delwood Sistrum."

"Accidents will happen, won't they? Oh I'll say they will, indeedy do." A chirping voice, tight smile. The man's hand caressed the dummy's seat.

"Didn't see, notice…"

"Not to worry, heh. I like these creatures too. Yesiree, you betcha boots. Can't talk back—not like the little woman eh, *eh?* Heh Heh." Tiny eyes glittering redly, hands writhing, mating snakes.

"She's dead," mumbled Horace. "Mum won't be saying anything more…"

"What?" replied Sistrum, placing the display model on a chair opposite Horace. One leg at right angles to the torso, pointed at Horace, the other was folded back crookedly under her buttocks. " *Dead?* For sure, this one is. Better dead than wed. That's what I always say. Little Christmas ho ho to brighten sir's day. To introduce myself: I'm Delwood Sistrum, Mr. Sistrum—my badge, you can see—head of Women's Lingerie. Perhaps sir is looking for?…"

But Horace wasn't listening. Somehow it was important to fix the model's legs, do *something* right. He tugged at her thighs. Customers whispering, pointing. Sistrum chattering.

"…Madam might like…just the thing…makes one's legs

21

daring, an invitation to..."

Silver slippers with stiletto heels were waved in his face. A sheer, black negligee appeared in the man's other hand.

"Little woman would adore...it's so, oh so naughty...removable..." Cherry eyes darting upwards, shoes and gown clutched to his chest.

Horace backed away. "No...thank you...won't need..."

"Then how about this?: the thigh-high calfskin and peek-a-boo lacies! Just think of the missus in..."

Horace was back in the mainstream of shoppers, then on the street again, walking, half running into the wind and driving snow. Another cab and he was home.

Someone in black was rapidly moving down the steps from the apartment building toward him.

"Karaki," said the man, vanishing into the whirling blizzard.

What had the detective been doing? Was he under suspicion? But he'd done nothing. And maybe that was just the whole trouble. He could see his tombstone now, the inscription: "In memoriam to Horace Stickle: The man who did absolutely nothing except die."

There was still time to change that, but it was running out. What had Futts said?: It was money in the bank? If so he might soon be overdrawn, in trouble. But not yet. His account was still open. Checks could be written. For a while anyhow. And that's what mattered, at least for the time being.

Later he woke up on the couch shivering and hungry, a large drink on the coffee table beside him. Eat, that's what he should do. Try and cook up something. But then he should try and do a lot of things, feel a lot of things. No energy, that was the problem. He felt drained, leaden. Not so much from the last few days, but months, maybe years. Things, shapes he couldn't define, hardly see, brushed against him at unexpected moments, made him sweat, tremble. Where was Ethel?: a meeting, executive conference on codes for etiquette enforcement? And Mum?: There she was still packaged on the end table. Get to her in a minute. First, though, a TV dinner into the microwave. "For Big Hungries", the label announced. A giant astride mountains grinned out at him from the cover.

Now for the football game he'd recorded on the video cassette. Amazing contraption. So what if the Adders had destroyed his Sunday afternoon by barging in with their pictures of a desert trip. His little gem had picked up the action.

Maybe he shouldn't unpackage the urn. Ethel might feel it an invasion of privacy. Wonder what had rattled? Just a peek to see...Damn. The string was knotted. Needed scissors. Why did he feel guilty? Not the same as opening a casket, defiling the dead, was it? There, a vase, small, grey, a screw-down top.

That wasn't the football...

"...Match of the decade friends: Tiny Tim versus Goblin Claus. Both these men...Midget wrestling at its best, brought to you by Brewbuster, the beer..."

Wrong station, sound blurred. He must have had the selector turned...Smoke, was that?...Why couldn't he remember the oven was microwave, not the other kind. Charred, a wrinkled cinder, the cremation of Chicken Little. Nothing resembling the golden delight on the package, not a meal for a Big Hungry at all. The giant glared at him from the garbage.

Come to think of it, how come people were supposed to turn into ashes, not something harder? — say coal or slag? Maybe that's what *actually* happened. Ashes were more poetic, a better sales product. He'd find out now. "Ready or not, Mum." Top immovable. Should use pliers, maybe a wrench. "One, two, *twist.*"

Powder, a fine whitish gruel with some pellets on top. Hold it up to the light and see just...Damn, all over the rug. How could he have dropped?...Lucky the urn hadn't broken. Strange looking ashes. Perhaps cremation left nothing suitable for containers, so fillers were used by those who manned the furnaces. Who would know? Did the bereaved, loved ones, ever open the urns, run the remains through their hands, gaze at the results of combustion? Probably not. Maybe some containers were even left empty for other use: a conversation piece, jar for candies, odds and ends. Who could tell what practices Katzenbach's used?

Ethel might look inside, though, expect contents, a sign of some kind. The broom and dustpan were useless. Better vacuum the stuff up into the Hoover, then empty the bag into

23

the urn. That was the best way. Plug it in over there, flick the switch. Something wrong. Clouds of Mum gusting into the air, his eyes and nose. Blasted machine blew, didn't suck. Must be the red button. Too late: powdery snow settling over furniture, drapes, his suit. A tingling in his nose, strange sensation. The spirit of Mum, expanding, trying to manifest itself, speaking to him? Ridiculous. But didn't the Bible speak of the Lord moving in mysterious ways, His wonders to behold? Maybe. But there wasn't anything magical about his nostrils, no treasure there, no passage to his soul. Best for now to empty the remains of the dust-bag into the urn, hope Ethel wasn't too curious. A drink, one more would be just...

Phone ringing. Perhaps Katzenbach's about the ashes, a mixup with flour instead of...

"We want the snow, man." Hoarse whisper.

"Snowman? You must have the wrong—"

"We're never wrong, Stickle, never. Ciao."

Crackpots. Should tie a dog whistle to the phone. Blast the galoots when they rang. Crank calls at all hours.

Lights flickering, fading. What breakdown this time at the nuclear plant, what poisons polluting the city, deforming future generations? Earthquake proof, a hundred percent safe, they'd said. Why then the brownouts, blackouts, outages, outrages, loss of power?: all the fancy terms to indicate it was candle time, back to basics. Tonight, though, there was no need for candles. Mr. Moon was on the job, a Chinaman with face aglow lamping the world.

Had he ever paddled Ethel on a northern lake, watched with her as sunset's fire touched rocky shores? A dream, another life, a different world. And dammit all, an Ethel that had died as surely as Mum Granger, a Horace Stickle who had had his brownouts too. But the lights would come on for him again, he'd see to it. You bet. He'd make an extra effort, do his job to perfection. No slip-ups. Mawsley would notice, Ethel too. He'd still get the promotion. That was the next step. And from there, who could tell? Things happened, sometimes good things. To him. The world would look different in the morning. It wasn't over by a long shot. Finish his drink, get some sleep.

Strange how the network of branches in the old tree seemed

to come alive in the moonlight: human outlines, silhouettes that motioned and nodded, danced to a foreign music.

Foreign music, shapes. His head acting up again. Well, so what if he'd like to shanghai a moonbeam and ride it to the stars, get the hell away from it all for a while? Who could blame him for that, who indeed?

4

"FOR ROBERTA AND KITTY, JOEL AND BUBBA—EARL
WRANGLER AND THE GOOBER COUNTRY CLAN WITH
SHE GOT THE GOLD MINE, I GOT THE SHAFT! HIT THAT
LITTLE BOOGER, EARL, LET'ER ROLL!"

What the?...Blasted radio—had he turned it on? Off now.

The vultures—were they still skreeching, arranging his
whitened bones to spell *snowman* on the desert sand? Had
Ethel really staked him out on an anthill? Mawsley covered
him with honey, whispered *shush*? Had?...

Eight-twenty? Late, never make it on time today. Objects,
himself, floating in a white haze. Haloes circling the bedposts,
lampshades. His face in the mirror blurring as if viewed through
cheesecloth. Hangover? Hadn't eaten dinner, that was it.
Breakfast...not much time. Time equalled money, job, not
food. Algebra equations, alphabet soup he'd never grasped.

"NOW OUR GOSPEL SPECIAL—REMINDIN' YOU ONCE
AGAIN THIS IS BIG RED FOR NIBBERS LITTLE LIVING
PILLS—ERLENE MUCKLUCK AND THE LIVIN' LORD
CHOIR HOLLERIN' FOR GAWD: *HALLELUJAH, I FOUND
SALVATION...*"

Damn radio, must've reset it. There, unplugged. A note under the TV dinner tray: "Meeting, left early. Urn to be *blue* not grey."

The chicken looked blacker and smaller than last night—lonely. Chopping block, oven and garbage—the coordinates of life for birdie. What a...

"...LOVELY WAY TO GO FRIENDS AND NEIGHBORS. IN HIS HANDS. NOW FOR WILD MAN SKEEGOG AND—"

"We interrupt regular programming for a brief newsbreak. In the Far East fighting has broken out between several countries. Authorities here consider it of minor importance at the present time.

"Now for our special: Flash Stud of Rolling Crud has just been arrested. Developments as they occur."

Hadn't he disconnected?...The urn, he'd return it at noon, straighten that out if nothing else. Other things—the radio—seemed beyond his power of control. Maybe he could make the eight-forty if he hurried.

"...*STOMPIN' MY BABY TO STONE*. HERE IT COMES, READY OR NOT. KILL HER SKEEGOG, MURDER THAT FIDDLE. YAHHOO!"

*

Futts coming out of *his* cubicle? Checking? It was only ten past nine. Damn, why couldn't he have made it in early the first day those sleuths were on the job. Futts saw him. That was good. No wave though, no morning "howdy" salute, just a nod, stare.

Felt as if he were walking uphill. The urn rolled to one side in his briefcase, the urn and his lunch. Ridiculous using a briefcase to transport a sandwich (and the only briefs he used were in his dresser). But he wasn't a nuts and bolts man, he was headquarters, white collar, briefcase material. His attaché case—yes, a classier symbol than briefcase—was his badge, the diploma he'd failed to get elsewhere. Look at the biggies, those with charisma and command presence: They had other insignia—sandboxes, curtains, windows, the thousand yard stare. You had to have some sign or you couldn't pass.

Futts had disappeared. No, back in the office, pate gleaming, thumbing a notebook. Should he smile, give with the hearty hello?

"Good morning, Mr. Futts. We have nothing to fear but fear itself." Had he said what he'd thought he'd heard?

"That's irrelevant, Stickle. Ivy League gibberish. Now I would like us—"

"Excuse, Mr.—"

"The name is Futts. *Mr.* Ripstrom Futts."

"Yes, I know. What I just said—slipped out. Don't know why..."

"You're *paid* to know. That's what it's all about: information, knowledge. To know is to fit. Ignorance is not bliss, Stickle, it's the other side of the mountain, downhill, a free fall to oblivion. Computers, communications, electronics, data processing, robotics, lasers, energetics, biochemistry, aerospace—it's a revolution, the new world. We don't use guns, bombs. It's microchips and processors, bytes and kilobytes, hardware, software—in short high-tech: HT. Information— the *right stuff*—is our ammunition, currency. Are you with me, Stickle?"

"Could I say—"

"The industrial revolution was fueled by energy. That's being replaced by the service sector, new industries fired by information, by the information society, the new capitalists— headmen—whose property snugs between the ears. Management needs to know what it wants immediately to make decisions, policy, in the interests of net profit. Are you familiar with Kahn's C^4I^2?: Command, control, communications, computing—information, intelligence? What do you know of Lisa the Mouse, Apple's new Peanut? Have you examined TRS— 80's, Pets? Are you?—"

"Mr. Futts, Mr. Battle was planning to have our personnel files put into some sort of computer program, but—"

"You mean to say you're still with *files*? That's square wheel, Stickle, caveman mentality. Amalgamated's global: oil, textiles, high-tech, smokestack—whatever. You're Personnel. How can management fit people into circles, squares, rhomboids, hectagons in a twinkling without computerization?

"Priddle, your colleague, *Mr.* Festin Priddle, has been taking night courses in computers, data processing, the works; keeping abreast of the future. Byte Magazine is on his desk. Managers, *assistant managers,* must have this expertise. It's not icing on the cake, it *is* the cake, the nitty gritty, gold at the end of the rainbow, in fact the very rainbow itself. You can slide into pots of success, have your cake and eat it too, but you must skip to the beat of the apocalypse. Are you tracking, Stickle? Have you seen the frontier, been pioneering with Priddle, ready to step up? Fill me in."

"Mr. Ripstrom—Futts—I didn't realize, know...Mr. Battle never asked that I take courses. Priddle never said anything about..."

"What you're trying to say, Mr. Stickle, is that you've become antiquated, not automated, in outlook."

"I don't really feel—"

"Not to interrupt, Stickle. What you *feel* is irrelevant. Hunch theory, winning friends to influence them, are boneyard. Versatility at the keyboard, technological command, is bottom line. To make your Pet sit up and talk, roll over, play dead, speak the word, the truth—that is the future, Stickle, upon us—you—today. You're a private in the knowledge proletariat, now. Work hard, you may get a stripe. Think about it. There isn't much time. It flies. So must I."

"Mr. Futts..."

Gone. What the hell was he supposed to do?: become an electronics wizard overnight? Bites, Pets, Apples and Peanuts—the dentist had criticized his overbite for years, and he was allergic to nuts: broke out in hives. Rude little man, Futts. Calling him Stickle. Knew Priddle's first name, though. Even put a *Mr.* before it. *Night courses,* Ethel and Priddle. Ethel had mentioned them several times, but he hadn't been listening. What had made him think she was making pottery or folk dancing?

The phone. Priddle no doubt scavenging for tidbits on Futts's visit. Must have been watching around the corner to see when he left.

"Medical? Yes, I...it had slipped my mind. Right away, I'll be there in a minute."

The yearly physical. Had the notice been sent a week ago? Maybe they could determine what was bothering him, advise what hardware—or was it software?—needed fixing.

That he didn't *feel* particularly good these days was important to him. That he had a feel for people, twenty-five years of *feel* in personnel seemed relevant. That the *feel* of someone stood above *fact* many times was significant—to him, anyway. Otherwise his career meant little, experience only excess baggage till Futts's headmen arrived, those prodigies who would step from school right into his shoes—his empty oxfords—to work the screens and blips, put him in the junkyard.

Futts just had to be wrong. When all was said and done, he and Joblobber would fold their tents and slip away in the night. Management would give token recognition to the Study, adopt one or two minor changes, and advise stockholders there'd been a major overhaul of corporate machinery. It'd happened before and would again: commotion without motion. Priddle on temporary assignment from corporate services would return, night courses and all, and, if the tumblers fell into place, the assistant manager's job would be his when Nordle retired next month. Let anyone deny he deserved it, anyone!

As the buzzer sounded, a light flashed on the medical scanner.

"Red Alert, Mr. Stickle. I'll have to get Doctor Foch."

"Red?...That noise, nurse, what does it mean? Am I?..."

The squeak of her rubber-soled shoes was already fading. The red light on the machine kept blinking, but the buzzer had gone off. Up till now the medical had gone smoothly. A mumble of voices rounded the corner.

"Helloalloallo. Yes indeed, a very good morning to you, Mr. Stingle, I'm Dr. Foch. Now..."

"It's Stickle, Doctor Foch."

"Of course it is. Let me have a squint here and..."

"Doctor, Red Alert, is? ...am?...just what?..."

"Means one or two major arteries are blocked, Mr. Stinckle. Very dangerous. Expiration on the spot is a possibility. Never lost one yet, though. Ho, whatya think of that? Odds are with you, my man. God's in his heaven, all's right with the world—for now."

31

"You mean...die, I might actually *die,* here, *now?*..."

"Makes you think, my boy, doesn't it? Thank your lucky stars for Solly the Scanner. She's a nuclear marvel, a veritable... Say, now what?—green. It's changing. Something outta whack. Nurse Parson, please get Stoney immediately."

"Doctor, could you tell me?..."

"We're busy, Mr. Stickle. Later. Can't you see something's wrong? It's obvious that...ah, the bell. Hear that ting bing ting. Means there's trouble somewhere. We have the yellow blinker now. Signals danger."

"My heart, though, Doctor Foch, am I in immediate?—"

"Danger? I should say so. Aren't we all? An oil slick here, a roller skate there; a loose screw, lunatics, things that go bump in the night. Do you believe in poltergeists, Mr. Stockly? I do. By golly, by jimbo, I could tell you...Ah, here comes Stone. If anyone can get to the bottom of this it's old Stoney."

"I hope so, Doctor Foch, my heart is beating terribly...."
Could the man with the cigar, tool kit strapped to his waist—the chap in the overalls and cap—be Stone? Why wasn't he wearing white, holding a clipboard, talking quietly?: someone who appeared capable of making his Pet do tricks? He looked drunk, seemed to be slurring his words.

"Sholly be on the Fritz, eh Doc? Lemmee see here. Giv'er a whack on the foundation bolts. Hmmm. Looketer go. She lit up like a Christmas tree now, by gar."

"Mr. Stone, I'm rather—"

"Eh? Who're you there?...Call me Chug. Always take the three beers for breakfast. Fuel 'er up on the suds first thing. Do that, you never sick. Yessiree, Chug gotter an A-1 engine under the ole hood. Now I'll be tightnin' this un, smack that inside nut over...Ha, musta been the quake, tremor. Shook up the head screw on Big Berta too. Whip'er on now, Doc. Think she be ok."

"Fine, that's the ticket, Stone. Don't know what we'd do without you. Everything's hunky-doo-dah, Mr. Starkle. You've got a green light. Small spot on the old melon, though. Normal wear and tear, my guess. Could be inflammation, the old nuteroo rebelling, mutant prostglandins, perhaps entropy—neurons on the run. Happens, you know: circuits overloaded, connections jammed, tremors in the brainpan. Red lights everywhere these days. Can't be helped. Might have Groat, Doc Groat down the street, have a look. I'll make an appointment. Groat's always got something up his sleeve. Till next time, Mr...."

"Stickle."

"Surely. Have a good one. Ciao."

"Nurse? This spot, is it, I mean?..."

"Not to worry, Mr. Stickle. Perhaps the tremor. Mr. Stone may not have tightened Solly completely. These things happen.

"You may come in, Mr. Priddle—Festin, isn't it? That will be all Mr. Stickle. You may go."

"Well well, Stickle old man. They called in Stone, I hear. A four alarm fire, eh? Can't live forever, dear boy. Gotta face it. Joblobber's been on safari for you. Tippytoes time. Say cheese, smile if you're cornered. Heads are rolling, tumbrils full. Yes indeed, times that try one's very soul. Looking lovely as usual, Nurse Parsons, even prettier than . . ."

On and on. He could hear the continuing drone of Priddle's voice through the closed door of the dressing room, the waiting room, in the corridor, at the elevators. Either Priddle's voice or echoes of it reverberating through his head, *melon* to Doctor Foch. What would Solly reveal sprocketing through Priddle's pumpkin?: a cartoon, midget wrestling, a cavalcade of lunatics. Why did the man seem obsessed with annoying him? Was he worried too? Had to be, taking night courses. Maybe he'd failed them, had health problems, would get the buzzer and red light. Did he have a wife, an Ethel? He'd have to put Priddle out of mind. Out of sight seemed impossible. The man was an oil slick that spread everywhere...

"Still hanging around, Stickle?"

"What?...*Priddle.*?"

"Yes, all through. Got the body of a teenager, eye of an eagle, mind of an Einstein, Stickle. They call me *Iron Boy* in there. Ciao."

The insufferable son of a...Be charitable, Horace Stickle. After all, he's only human. Try and see the good, his virtues. But dammit all, he couldn't. And strive as he might to erase it, an image arose of Priddle stepping for an elevator that wasn't there. He could even hear his screams of "ciao" as the man cartwheeled through endless shafts of empty space while

33

buzzers and bells and flashing red lights accompanied his fading cries.

*

Was his office on fire? From down the hall, he could see wisps of smoke curling against the glass partition, then the back of a head. Joblobber, if he wasn't mistaken. Must be. There was the pipe, wavelets of steel-grey hair, now the profile of the man himself. Better news than Futts. Joblobber had an air of understanding, the fatherly twinkle in his eye. He'd see through Priddle, recognize merit and advise it be rewarded. Think positive, it always worked—usually.

"Mr. Stickle, top of the morning to you, sir. Have a seat."

"Mr. Job—"

"Call me Bob, most folks do. Bob Joblobber: a full course meal, eh?"

"Yes, of course, Mr. —Bob. Just had my yearly medical. Usually am in my office. Hope you didn't have to wait very?..."

"Not to worry, not at all. These interruptions happen, cut into efficiency, alas; but they're just another challenge, are they not, Mr. Stickle, obstacles to overcome?"

"Well, I suppose..."

Should he sit behind the desk? Didn't seem proper; after all, he was being interviewed.

"Pull up a chair. Would you like a cigar? Here, try one of these. Prefer the pipe, myself. Allow me. New lighter; fires every time; transistorized, I think."

"Thank you ...not used to...very good..."

Blasted thing had almost shot out of his mouth. Why couldn't he have said *no*. Had he ever smoked one? Felt as if he were rolling a small log between his lips. He should have sat down behind his desk. The metal chair in the corner bit into his thighs, tilted to one side. Shreds of tobacco stuck to his tongue, and his lungs burned. Joblobber smiled, gazed at the ceiling and drew deeply at the pipe. Little donuts floated toward him. He closed one eye and squinted through the holes coming closer. Bob's mouth was moving, talking, working again and again at the pipestem.

"...And so, I'd be most interested in hearing your thoughts."

34

"Pardon, fine, well I…"

"Retraining, early retirement, the end of the line—it's all a bit unsettling isn't it, Horace? I should think so. You can speak freely with me, though, as a *paisan*, a…a sort of comrade-in-arms. Perhaps a touch of this might help, oil the old tongue. Be my guest."

"I don't really…but, certainly generous; perhaps just a small…"

The flask, silver, leather tooled. His blasted hand was trembling as he took it, poured. Had he ever tasted anything so smooth?: a coffee-whiskey blend that kept going down and down and…"Early…did you say *retirement*? Joke, Bob? Ho. The gold clock and all that; certainly not something…"

Couldn't remember what he'd been about to say. The alcohol was first warmth, then a bonfire quickly spreading from his stomach to all parts of his body. The two fingers holding the cigar felt numb, then his whole hand, now his face. Ashes dropped onto his pants and drifted to the floor. A couple of deep puffs might steady him. Lips numb. Had flame speared from the end of the cigar?

Priddle's face was glued to the glass partition. He tipped his cigar to him and grinned. Had that bellow of laughter been his. Joblobber was smiling. Why not? Solly had been wrong: It'd been green, not red; no buzzers and bells, not the red light for Horace Stickle.

His stomach ached from laughing or alcohol. Priddle's face was the size of a marble, then gone. Could Joblobber be frowning? Had the smile disappeared? "Mr. Jolly Bob…Job…" Tongue in knots, voice tiny, a cry from across a lake or distant cliffs. Blow smoke rings, show Jober he had class too, could puff curlicues with the best of them.

"Quite a mouthful, isn't it?—the name. Never mind, Horace. I gather, ah, the early retirement idea doesn't appeal, that you find it rather ludicrous. Am I correct? After all, many of us would enjoy getting on with the second, even third acts of our lives. But then today's idealists, the real ones, Horace, are the materialists, the new entrepreneurs in scuffed shoes and open shirts, who invent, take risks, build new enterprises and create employment; who jump off mountains and hope the parachute will open. Yes indeed, the business world is the diamond of occupations; but there are other fields—"

"Not for my father, Bob. There wasn't anything else. Business was the only mountain to climb for him."

Oh that Neldroon Stickle could see him now: the chair tilted back, his son talking turkey to a top executive over smokes and morning whiskey. Joblobber was smiling again. "Do you really think, Robert, that commerce is the leading activity of mankind, perhaps of extraterrestrial beings throughout the universe? Are they all out there in the stardust with charts and graphs discussing bottom lines and earned surplus, the bulls and the bears?—little green men with antennae sticking out of their heads buying and selling moons and stars?

"Is there a Wall Street of the Milky Way, Mr. Joblobber (his tongue agile as a snake now, ideas a cascade of crystal rain pouring into his brain), a Universal Stock Exchange, a Fortune's Five Hundred of the solar system."

"Very poetic, Horace. Yes, of course, we're all transacting for profit of one kind or another, aren't we? Ho, even with the Devil. Your father, is he still alive? What line of endeavour was he associated with?"

"Neldroon passed on several years ago. Held a number of franchises in the Burger Bomb chain. Tragic at the end: choked testing the specialty of the House, a Hiroshima Blast: three quarters of a pound of beef between two buns big as catchers' mitts. Died in harness though, on the job, just as he always wanted."

"What do *you* want, Horace? What is *your* dream? Company has to take account of all these things. We must have a complete profile, consider heart as well as head. Sleep on it, my boy. Get your pidgeons on parade. We'll talk again. Festin—your colleague, Festin Priddle—is next. Invited me to lunch at *Belle Époque*. Till later. Enjoy."

"But Bob, Mister..."

Waving to him over his shoulder? No, to someone else— Priddle—hovering a few feet down the hallway. Had he been lurking out there all the time, spying, listening? How long had the front legs of the chair been digging into the top of his shoes? To rise, he'd have to tilt back...

"I say, Mr. Stickle, are we on the job this morning? Almost

missed you in the corner there, hmmm. Smoking, I see. Can kill you, my dear man. A filthy habit, and a cigar at that."

"Miss Mousey, I mean, Mawskey..."

Damn chair had really pinned his feet. Had to stand up. She was a woman, or was?...Numb, collapsing...on his knees...

"Mister Stickle, I do not demand *that* sort of recognition. Up up. Here, take my—"

"*There* you are Harriet...I say, Horace—er, Mr. Stickle— what in *heavens*?... You look positively grey."

"I told him, Ethel, standing is sufficient, kneeling is quite unnecessary. Ho, just a morning funny, Mr. Stickle. Carry on, keep smiling. It isn't over yet, is it? Have a good one."

Lips loose, rubbery. *Grey?*—him? No *blue*, the urn was to be blue. He'd get on with that and lunch. Things would go better in the afternoon, they usually did.

5

THERE IT WAS, in black script on the sign: *Katzenbach's Parlor— Quality With Taste And Economy.* A neon angel with harp blinked above the door. Several bulbs were dead. Chimes gonged at his touch on the bell, the door swinging inward, then swishing shut as he entered. Fluttering curtains, a head poking out. Now a tug at his pantcuff, teeth needling his leg.

"*Ralph.*" A whisper. "*Come, come here.*"

Then a squeal as the creature went for his foot, the mouth a red lifesaver gnawing his shoe. A hand at the curtain clenching a bone, waving it slowly. Good, the animal racing away. A rustle behind him, then the man, a steeple in black.

"You rang, sir? Too late, I'm afraid, for today."

Voice, a murmur, far overhead; face, a pale moon gliding by and then gone. Arguing voices, a shout, the yelp of a dog down the hall. Door slamming and footsteps, the hum of a choir. Two men in work clothes and caps passing by. "Excuse me, could you?..."

"Freezer, she be on hold down below. Need an A-Pipe Disjoint to fix 'er." Burst of laughter, on out the door.

A bulge at the curtain, then bustling through in curlers and mules, a short stocky woman blowing her nose.

"Busy, so terribly...nothing right...I'm sorry...Where's Fred? Fred, *Fred!*"

"Ma'm, two men just left..."

"Them was Red and Lon, sweet. They's way behind on the boxes. Freezer was thawin'; everythin' 'bout to go bad. It's just nothin's right today—anyday. Now, you'd be...Have to hurry, I just don't..."

"It's the urn, this one. My wife asked for blue, but as you can see..."

"Your name, I didn't catch?..."

"Stickle, Horace—"

"Yes, that's nice. Color blind. Got the 'ritis, bunions too. Tell you, some days it aint worth rollin' outa bed. Be plantin' me soon, the way I feel. Yes, I—"

"That's too bad...Another thing, the urn didn't seem to contain ashes and—"

"Foulups. Happen all the time these days. Whole shebang bein' switched to computers for transfers, burnin's, boxin's, transplants. Even had stuff from Happy Huntin' Pet Home come in here. Tremors the other day knocked out the power. Couldn't light the fires, got backlogged. I'm fillin' in for Ester. Name's Edna. Don't know too much 'bout all this. Guzman, he—"

"Guzman? That was who handled Mum, Mrs. Granger. He gave me the urn. He'd know..."

"Snoram? He's out now. Detective was in here a while back: Kracky, or sumpin. Wanted to talk to Snoram about—"

"Detective Karaki? I know him. He—"

"The less I know, the better, dearie. Get what I mean? Raldo asked 'bout everything. Always with the questions. He's gone. Accident in the cellars. Snoram, he wants to hook up all the Homes in the state—country—to this computer thing. Turn the buryin' business into a regular discount flea market. Insult to the dead, I say. No respect..."

"You're quite right, but—"

"Gotta light? Thanks. Had others in here complainin' last week or two. Still can't match up the ashes. Lost some in the trash. I'll tell Guzman. He'll phone..."

40

"Thank you, but about the urn, blue..."

"AND NOW *THE WALBASH CANNONBALL* BY WILD MAN SKEEGOG..."

"Shorty, I told you, that's comin' down here! It's the other dial! *Turn...* Them containers, urnals, do we have any in blue or?—"

"AH GOT MAH BABY..."

"Damn man couldn't find his face with both hands if'n he was starvin'. Check back in a day or two, would you. Ester'll know. Gotta run. Ciao."

"But, it's important..."

"FLASH STUD OF CRUD..."

"When will I?..." The tall man in black taking his arm firmly, leading him to the door.

"The Toweletts are in procession." Voice low, breathless. "A Necropolis Special. To be consumed in the Rolls. May He give you a good one."

Outside, the door closing. Lights rippling over the angel's harp, snow sifting through an iron-pot sky.

" Fa la la la la, la la la la. Drink Brewbuster, folks, and find heaven on earth. All you ever wanted out of life and more. Deck the halls with..."

Blasted truck, right through the red light. Slush all over his shoes, almost killed..."Idiot, bloody fool!"

Look at the driver, giving him the finger. A snowball, he'd throw...barely missed. Serve the damn guy right if...Oh Jesus, was that?...not a police car? Had it hit?...The siren...Did the cop see who?..."Cabbie, cabbie!" Stopping, lucky. Now if only..."To Amalgamated. Fast, it's an emergency. We haven't time."

"Amalgamated what, Sammy?"

"Sorry, *Food*, Amalgamated Foods. I work there. It's my lunch..."

The man had slammed a glass divider shut, didn't want to hear him. Could block out most everything, be his own boss. Maybe he should hack a cab. The word *hack* had a tough crack to it. Yes, with plaid cap, leather jacket, the aviation sunglasses and cigar like the driver, he'd fit the role, be a real hacker. A man's work, bit of danger involved. Always muggers and killers on the prowl. He'd carry a gun in the glove compartment. No, stuck in his belt. A hunting knife might come in handy too. He'd learn judo, kung fu, the martial arts—become a lethal weapon, a man like...

Must be a mistake on the cabby's I.D. pasted to the partition: *Ursula Ranger, Female, 5'11", white caucasian...* Was that his stomach?: a squeal, not even a manly growl. Could it all be a conspiracy?: a plot to rid the world of mankind, establish a matriarchy?

Would Mum Granger, a female Lazarus, materialize from the urn if he rubbed it, return to lead a women's world? Dressed in leather and jack boots, would they ensure men ended up in zoos, became beasts of burden, obsolete? Could it be revenge, not equality hovering in the wings?

Yet had men ever really wanted to be kings of the various castles anyway? Or was it all a myth, a self-deluding legend based on vanity of size, muscle? Maybe the Mums and Mizes were giving the men an honorable discharge, taking over what a lot of them never wanted in the first place: the grind from nine to five and beyond. Only a matter of time till women saw the trap, and then what?: split the difference with men? let the computers and robots take over? Was that the future?: everyday a holiday, an endless vacation where little mattered?

Could that be?...Priddle alright, coming out of *Belle Époque*, Joblobber clapping him on the shoulder. Oh that Brewbuster would give Priddle a soaker; that he dared hurl Mum at Priddle's Daniel Boone coonskin; that he be anyone else but Horace Stickle just for a day, today. But most of all, oh that God grant him the strength to survive till he could pick up a Monster sub from Pig-Out, the new deli across from Company.

"Watcha got in there, Stickle?: the corpus delicious? Heh heh."

"Lunch, Priddle. Not all of us can afford fancy restaurants."

"Few of us have the stomach for that carnival of garbage the deli concocts. Smells, Stickle. Reeks of kennels, worse. If I were you...ah, Messrs. Joblobber and Futts on the runway. Offer them a bite. Maybe they'll recommend you for chef."

42

Priddle would *have* to be in his office, catch him going by. Should have eaten at the deli, but lunch hour was over. And now just what he'd hoped to avoid—interruptions before he could get to his office and dispose of the sandwich.

"Mr. Stickle, we were looking for you. Never tag you at home plate. Have a little something to discuss...Festin, delightful meal."

"Thanks Bob. Maybe tomorrow? Mr. Futts, perhaps you would like to join..."

"Eat on the run. Time equals money equals profit if used wisely. Live on Spirula, sea food capsules."

"You don't say. Bought some myself the other day. Newest thing in the health food market. Keep them in my desk drawer. Here, have a couple."

"Hmmm. I like a man on top of his health, Mr? ..."

"Festin, Festin Priddle."

"To never forget: the bottom line is health. Lose that, time's up, and you push dirt or the tin cup. Stickle, that brings me to you. You—"

"Ah, Ripstrom, perhaps I should carry the ball on fourth and short. Gentlemen, due to rather severe weather systems moving in quickly, if you get my drift, we've had to act quickly to implement Company's new strategic and tactical policies; retarget their trajectory to maximize objectives conducive to stabilizing and, of course, establishing leadership in the field. Taking into account economic, and especially human factors, some changes in work place organization and functions of work persons will be required to optimize input and output of staff support roles. This means—"

"To cinch the knot, Stickle, Festin here, and Crewshaw will complete computerization of files. Plummer and Rumsey will rotate to Personnel Services. That leaves you, Stickle, with nothing."

"But Mr. Futts—"

"To finish, Stickle. For you it is not discharge or layoff, but—"

"*Fired*, you're saying?—"

"To repeat, *not* discharge, but 'In-house', 'Out-house', retraining. You will study Apple, Mouse, theory. The circuitry of Chip, artificial intelligence, biochipping, transmorgs—living

43

chip in the brain yoked to computer process."

"*Outhouse...retraining...* I've been through every section in personnel, Mr. Futts. Twenty-five years—"

"You're making noise, Stickle, not sense. Without the codes, rules, we can't communicate, evolve, do anything. Too many, we moulder; too few, it's a free-for-all, asylum time. Entropy either way. The code is changing, Stickle: new rules, lines of communication, relationships. You must reset your compass, take other bearings. You're in a different time zone. Speed traps abound. Pedal to the floor, brake—it's a matter of balance. Lose it?: arrest, jail, perhaps Chair. Company has given its plasma, lifeblood, profit, for a quarter century toward your welfare, happiness. For that you owe. Repayment is due. You must readapt, give—"

"Let me go long on this one, Ripstrom. Mr. Stickle, there's a wonderful new circus in town. New acts, funnier clowns and more daring acts. The industrial revolution took over a couple of a hundred years to peak. But the information revolution has come to the fore in barely thirty. Information is the key resource of the future, not scarce or nonrenewable, but expandable. Information technologies, communications, post-industrial society—the information society—requires new skills, outlooks: a reshaping of individual, cultural, political and economic visions.

"Leaders of the new elite will not so much control or own traditional property and production forces as be capable of managing and assessing the information upon which decisions are made involving these things. Now, Horace, all this may take a moment or two to sink in, but—"

"May I say, Mr..."

"Call me, Bob, Festin."

"Thank you, Bob. Everything you say is absolutely on the money. As clear as— Excuse, Mr. Futts, you were going to—"

"Wasting time. Stickle, you still seem unglued. Something more?"

"*More.* Mr. Futts, I could spend all day...Where do I fit in now? What responsibilities?..."

"I'll take that handoff, Ripstrom. You'll be pleased, I'm sure, Mr. Stickle, to learn that during computer retraining we've managed to keep you payrolled, benefits continuing, as

44

a Produce Engineer Grade Four at Amalgamated's largest local emporium at Stamper and Groine—Pig-Wig. Pay's less, but then, hmmm, so's the job. Bit of lifting, shoving of carts, boxes—that sort of thing. Do you a world of good, the exercise, running around. Need more of it myself, by jimminy, I surely—"

"*Produce engineer.* You must be!...*emporium,* the *store, food...*"

"Thought you'd be gung ho. Well off—"

"*Lifting boxes, shoving? Computer retraining?...* Mr. Joblobber, every aptitude test I ever took showed up poorly for mechanical or technical ability. I have no interest...I'm good with people. I can relate to human beings, not graphs of them on screens, not as numbers on a keyboard. There's no feeling there. That's working with things, with...with ghosts, not people."

"That's the idea, Mr. Stickle; Company will make a new man out of you, broaden your horizons, deepen your keel. Sky's the limit. It's a marvelous zip bang world out there, yours for the taking. Indeed indeed. Now Festin, about this evening..."

*

This evening, Festin. Another meal? A night at the opera? Priddle not only had his foot in the door, but everything else as well, including his luggage. Better eat lunch, tidy up leftover odds-and-ends. His final meal, the last supper. Spread the Monster out on his desk and...Damn thing was slipping, spilling over his shoes, floor, pants...

"That him, Offsuh! He duh one! He done it! Dat Pickle! Tryda rape me!...steal!..."

"Lady, will you please?...Are you a Horace Pickle? Information downstairs said Prickle."

"No, I'm Stickle."

"I tole you, Offsuh, he done it...See, he's 'Malgamated, ahrite..."

"Mrs. Vanders has filed a complaint. There are witnesses—"

"Miz *Flossie* Vanders, wife of Roan, you heah, Pickle."

"I'm afraid I'll have to serve you with these, Mr. Stickle. Will you just sign here?"

"Let me see those..."

Feet slipping as he moved, skidding apart on the fillers and mayonnaise, throwing him sideways into the officer. Both of them on the floor.

"I gets him. That mouse mine. Tryin' a git out, 'scape."

The woman, grizzly black, loomed above, shopping bag raised. Crimson filmed his eyes. Oh that he had a gun, a bomb, that could pulverize them all: Futts, Joblobber, the gigantic negress about to strike, the officer thrashing on top of him, likely going for his gun. Better still, give him a weapon that would explode Amalgamated into rubble and dust, demolish it forever...

"Hello hello hello. Mr.Stickle, a problem? Can I?..."

"No, Miz Mawsley, it's just a misunderst—"

"To remind, Mr. Stickle. Store tomorrow. All hunky-doo."

"Miz Mawsley, I cannot understand why after twenty-five years?..." Lettuce and fillers hanging from his hands. Hard to rise. The officer staring at him.

"The papers are on your desk, Stickle. Come, Mrs. Vanders, there was no need to accompany—"

"Ise sees you in the poahhouse, Pickle. We's suing too, everythin'. Jes you wait, rich boy. Roan gonna fix you good."

"Are you sure, Mr. Stickle, you don't need?..."

"No, thank you, Miz Mawsley, a personal matter..."

"Must tend to those little things at home, mustn't we. Twenty-five years, you say. A lot to be grateful for. Indeed it is. And more to come. Think of that, the future beckons. Pack it up for the day, Mr. Stickle. Celebrate. The best is before you."

"Miz Mawsley—"

"Must fly, take a meeting and—Hello, you would be?..."

"Priddle, *Festin* Priddle. Most attractive dress, Miz Mawsley. It has...such flair."

"Thank you, Fes...Mr. Priddle. Something I whipped up myself. Natural, textured burlap with...Must hurry. My office, Mr. Priddle. About four? I like to get to know my people. Ciao."

"Good day, Miz Mawsley. Four it is. Gardening, Stickle? Or do you eat off the floor? Heh."

"Priddle, I've had just about enough..."

"Maybe you're practicing up for the store. Lots of food to play around with in there. Why you could—"

"Shut up, do you hear me, Priddle, you godda—"

"*Mr. Stickle.* I've warned you about that before!"

"*Ethel,* what the?..."

"*Miz Trench*, the name is Miz Trench, Mr. Stickle. Harriet said you'd left for the day. Mr. Priddle has requested *this* office!"

"Thank you, Ethel, Miz Trench. I must say that hairdo is most—very today. Has that...that flourish..."

"How nice of you, Festin. Just a little creation of my own.

"Mr. Stickle, please clean up the floor for Mr. Priddle before you leave. Ta."

"Yes, Stickle, the place is rather a piggery. Hop to it, old man. I'll be by in a jot or two."

"Priddle, a trough would be absolutely ideal for you..."

Grinning at him through the glass, cupping his ear. The man wasn't worth the rage welling inside, the violent images of destruction: Priddle in flames, on a spit, screaming from a cauldron, his head shattered, contents a vegetable stew on the floor before him.

No it wasn't Priddle that infuriated, something with more size. Injustice? Who expected fairness, though? Well, he did, a bit anyway. But it was beyond that. As if he were swimming in the ocean and suddenly glimpsed the dark of giant shapes rising from the depths, disappearing, surfacing and then mounding at the horizon over which they slipped. Perhaps without warning he would ascend on the back of one of those creatures, be borne aloft for an instant, then swallowed whole or flung into oblivion.

Celebrate, go home. Wasn't that what Mawsley'd said? Why not? Take a cab. Maybe early retirement *was* best. *Produce Engineer:* white collar no more, turning gray fast, like Mum's urn. What if neighbors, other headquarters' people, saw him piling soup, carting? Best hang in there for now, though. Something would happen. It wasn't over yet. He'd make his mark.

Had that been a tremor, a dimming of light? Maybe his own foundations were loose, crumbling, a case of terminal brownout. Something to consider, another shadow on the wall.

47

6

"THE BATTLE ARMS Apartments, please, on Rostow."

This cabbie was definitely a man, unless it was a *she* with beard. Could it be only two-thirty in the afternoon? Sky dark with streaks of silver zigzagging the horizon.

"Strange, lightning this time of year."

"Pardon, mister?"

"Sky so black. Guess we're in for a blizzard."

"First time she's been blue in days. Guess you're lookin' at something else."

"*Blue?* Must've dozed off, imagined..."

The black was fading quickly now, sun shining, sky clear. Why was it he felt vaguely guilty, disgusted with himself, in a way tainted? For an instant at the office, he'd wanted to smash Priddle, attack the cop, inflict pain and destruction. Had he ever felt that way before? Not so strongly, not with such— what?—hatred, sense of...*enjoyment*? Hard to figure. He didn't hate the policeman, just doing his job. Priddle, was a nitwit, a clever one, but insufficient to arouse loathing. Maybe the Vanders woman calling him a mouse—filthy little creatures —had something to do with it.

Hadn't he read somewhere that it was the mice, the no-bodies, those who saw themselves as useless, who made concentration camps possible, who lit the ovens and manned the firing squads, in fact stood for Evil. Perhaps others were included: fanatics, sure; and everyone who had a...a feeling, instinct, for right and wrong—no it was more than that—for good and evil, and gave in, defied the good because—why?: they were scared, thrilled to pain, violence? Just didn't care?

Was he one of *them*?: a small man with the heart of a rat and diseased soul? Was that what he sensed, hatred of himself because he feared failure, impending zeroness; because he had seen those twisted shapes that coiled his heart: phantoms of a dark and brutal deep he'd never sensed before.

"This is close enough, think I'll walk from here. Thanks. Here—no, keep the change. Crazy to ask, but they say cabbies know a lot of things. Any idea what it means to be brave, not a coward, I mean?"

"Brave? Couldn't tell you. Been sort of fearful—well not really that: let's say living with the *awareness* of fear all my life. Was in the war. Frightened as hell most of the time. Never understood why they gave me a medal for wiping out a pillbox. So scared that time I did everything you could and more in my pants. Afterwards shook for hours. Always worried about getting mugged in the cab. Take your money, then waste you for kicks. No, I'm not the man to ask about *brave*. Maybe it's cowards who don't run. Hell man, I don't know. Take it easy now, hear."

Half a block to the apartment. Cold air made him shudder. Trees, bare—witches with a thousand arms, their fingers pointing, bony, gnarled, accusing him. The man in the black overcoat and hat coming from the Battle Arms had stopped on the front steps, was staring his way. Dammit, Detective Karaki. Maybe he could turn back, escape. Too late, Karaki had moved. Suddenly he was off the steps, down the walkway and gliding towards him on the sidewalk, a black cat on its hind legs closing fast.

"Afternoon, Mr. Stickle, Your office said you'd left early. A couple of things to discuss."

Had the man spoken? Lips motionless, gaze fixed above, beyond, him; no doubt riveted on the trees, their signal of

50

guilt. "Mr. Karaki, please excuse...It's been a terrible day. I'm not well. Can't this wait?"

"Wait, wait for what, Mr. Stickle?: till things get better? They never do, you know. The engines of rust and rot are at full throttle. Termites, nits, the sucks and crawls are on overtime, have been since He created His smorgasbord of wonders. One day that big lightbulb up there will, *splink,* go out, and we'll all hang from the planet frozen, icicles in a black night rushing toward oblivion. Everyone knows that.

"But on to more important matters. The autopsy report, Mr. Stickle, indicates that Mrs. Granger's death was caused by a *blow* to the back of the head. Now..."

"*Blow,* Detective Karaki? Did the bathtub rise up and strike her? She slipped and hit her own head. *She,* Mr. Karaki, *Mum Granger,* hit her *own* head all by herself. *Herself,* do you hear me, all by *herself.*"

"You seem excited, Mr. Stickle. Why are you so eager to blame Mrs. Granger? Most certainly she didn't intentionally bash her brains out, did she?"

"Look—"

"Not to interrupt. Furthermore, there was a scream, loud yelling after that. Explanations?"

"Karaki, listen—"

"*Detective* Karaki, Mr. Stickle, *Detective.*"

"Of course. Detective Karaki, I was in our livingroom with a beer, reading the evening paper, when I thought I heard the scream—shout. It wasn't that loud. The bathroom door was shut, my wife was using a blender. I went down the hall to tell her dinner was ready and—"

"To tell her about *dinner,* Mr. Stickle, not to investigate the scream? And the yelling?"

"We thought she might have fallen asleep in the bath, or been on the toilet. Constipation. Won't talk to anybody then. But dinner was on the table. My wife yelled; Mum wouldn't answer."

"I see, A most powerful blow to the bathroom door. For a man your size, you must be very strong."

"No, Ethel did that. Studies karate."

"People next door—two men, a Futts and Joblobber, I believe—said the outcries were clearly audible."

"*Futts and?*...I don't know the layout of their apartment. Maybe our bathroom is next to their livingroom or bedroom or bathroom. What *is* all this, Detective Karaki—these questions? You can't possibly be suggesting, thinking, *I* killed Mum Granger? Why that's so, so..."

"So *what,* Mr. Stickle? Many men dislike their mothers-in-law, even hate them, would love to get rid of them. Did she visit you a lot, crowd the apartment, gang up on you with your wife? Are you having problems at work, losing promotions? Do you feel insecure? Was Mrs. Granger a nag? Did she pick at your failures, visit on short notice and stay indefinitely? Did she, Mr. Stickle? Was she such a pestilence that sometimes you wished you could obliterate her and wipe her jeers and sneers from the face of this planet? In a fit of a rage did you splinter the door and put out her bulb forever and ever? —send your Mums pell mell into the darkness? You did, Mr. Stickle, didn't you? Violence triumphed, crime prevailed. For once you were the mouse that roared instead of squealed. Am I right, Mr. Stickle? Are you not guilty? We all are, you know, every last one of His creatures.

"Would you believe I've imagined my *own* mother-in-law, Mother Trap, in a pit of bubbling lava. But I'd never *put* her there. No, definitely not; that would be murder. And I'd burn along side her in Hell for all eternity after being electrocuted. I repeat, Mr. Stickle, are you guilty of?—"

"Of *course* I'm guilty of the most terrible atrocities, Detective Karaki! I almost caved in a policeman's face with a dangerous projectile today, tried to attack a beer truck. Were it possible, I'd've used bombs, anything, to destroy people and property this very afternoon. I'm the perfect type to run concentration camps, cheer when the smoke pours from the chimneys. Job, problems?: They want me to push carts, turn my job over to an electronic mouse. All this after twenty-five years, a quarter of a century. Mum Granger—her ashes, urn, the woman's ghost—is still after me. My wife—*Mum's daughter*—has ordered I call her *Miz*! My wife! *Guilty?*: Is that the right word? Sure, why not? I'm as guilty—"

"Thank you, Mr. Stickle, Rod has it all down. Not to fear you'll be misquoted at the appropriate time."

"*Rod?* What *time*?"

"My mini Pet, Mr. Stickle. Take it everywhere. Useful at trials, hearings."

"*Trials...*"

Had Karaki flashed something at him?: a tiny oval glinting in his palm? The man was coasting away, at the corner, rounding Bone Street, gone. *My rod and my staff they comfort me.* Wasn't that from the Bible? And Karaki had talked of Mum as a "pestilence." That had a scriptural flavor too. Something about not being afraid of the pestilence that walked in darkness and the destruction that wasted you at noon.

Well, it was afternoon now, and nothing had happened. But still, the sky was black, threatening storm, perhaps a monumental blizzard that would bury the city, waste *it* in hundreds of feet of ice and snow, turn them all into frozen swizzle sticks, the ultimate pestilence, brownout, that would no doubt lie beyond the healing powers of walking canes or rods or anything else.

***

Was that the phone? Had he entered the building, come up the elevator, unlocked the door and walked into his apartment? Odd that he was in his pajamas. Seemed as if he were in a dream. Someone else's. The continuing jangle must indeed be the phone—that, or an alarm tripped in his head.

"We want it back, Stickle." Voice hoarse, demanding.

"Pardon, hello. Who is this?"

"*Who*, isn't important. *It*, is. Don't play games, Stickle. We'll close you down, put shutters on your candy store. Ciao."

"Hello, *hello...*"

Buzzing, line dead. *Games, it?* Had someone actually talked, whispered from the phone receiver in his hand? Imagination?: the wind at the windows?

Chicken Delight from last night stared blackly from the table, its charred corpse more shrivelled since morning. Was that measled green thing in the frig an orange? Those strands worming the plate at the back must be the rutabaga from Mum night. And that quivering mess by his hand?—consommé, a brownout to be sure. Nothing else but diet beer, some wine: a no-collar larder for sure.

"Pig-Out? Yes, this is Mr. Stickle at the Battle Arms Apart-

ments on Rostow. You deliver? Fine. One Monster, one pizza
—a Whammo. Pardon? Apartment eleven sixty-six. Thank you."

He'd finish the beer, wine too. Damn, not wine, vinegar.
Terrible, could pucker a drain. Was that sheet lightning? The
room shimmered in a milky haze, all melting, swimming
together in white waves that flowed toward him. Tired,
hungry...oh for the Monster and Whammo, the Monster and...

Ah, there it was floating toward him out of the clouds, a
huge blimp chock full of salami, pepperoni, shards of lettuce,
layers of tomatoes and cheeses, all trailing the delicate perfume
of oils and spices in which his palate would find utopia. Delay
the ecstasy for an instant, peek inside to glimpse the treasure
and...*Priddle*, amidst the goodies, pounding drums, no a
keyboard, computer, that spewed a staccato crescendo
of noise...

"...Home, Mr. Stickle, a Stickle?...Whammo, Monster!
Pig-Out delivery! PIG-OUT!"

"Coming, I'm here. Here I am. Asleep. Sorry, dozed..."

"Twelve dollars, Mr. Stickle, and whatever else...Very
cold out there, you know..."

"Yes, to be sure. Keep the change. Thank you."

Damn, he'd given the man two tens. Thought it'd been a ten
and a five. Strange, he'd resembled someone—the woman
cabby? lady at the funeral home? Now for Monster. Aroma
from Whammo tingled his eyes, sharpened the room, bathed
it in an ivory sheen. Perhaps things would work out. He'd
phone about the urn tomorrow. Poor old Mum, tucked away
in a jar, ashes no doubt mixed up with those of an animal, bird,
reptile, even possibly an insect, a large one. He should paint
the grey urn blue. That would save a lot of trouble. Thirsty.
Time for a cold beer and then back to food.

That crunch?—underneath him as he'd sat down with the
beer. *Damn*, right on his briefcase. Why hadn't he bought the
solid bulky model rather than the executive Razorback? *For
The Man With The Million Dollar Mind*, the advertisement
had stated, displaying a distinguished gentleman removing a
check for that amount. Dust smoking from the open zipper,
the urn in pieces, room blurring. No longer hungry, forehead
burning. Who was it Doctor Foch had suggested seeing?:
Goat, Groat? He'd make an appointment tomorrow and...But

he'd be at the store.

Store. How many times had he heard headquarters' people refer to the office as *shop, store?* A usage perhaps to obscure the fact their work lacked—what?: grease and spit?—life? If Futts had his way, headquarters' people might indeed be entirely replaced by amazing machines run by lumps of coal, charred chickens, the remains of...He could will his body to the city, stipulate it be used to energize the waterworks, light the lamps, power the generators. He'd be used up completely. Burn with a fire that would ignite the world, an eternal flame...

Asleep, awake?—he drifted silently among the stars, a glitter-blur through which a silver mask grinned down at him, a Priddle face that zoomed in near and disappeared. And then a whiteness hovering close: a shape, a gown and angel wings, the halo sparkling, blinking out a message with His starry jewels. Clearer, brighter, yes there it was, the very word of God Himself...*HORACE STICKLE PRODUCE ENGINEER GRADE FOUR.*

The cherub glowed, then burst aflame. And from the fire came neon Mum with urn in hand to hound him through the darkening night.

7

"...AND IT'S *GO GETTUM* TIME! UP AND AT 'EM FOLKS.
ANOTHER LOVELY MORNING HERE AT *W.R.A.T.*...
WRAAHHT! YOUR HOST FOR THE NEXT FOUR HOURS,
LITTLE OLE ME, BIG BOMBERMAN, SPINNIN' THE WINNAHS.
AND NOW..."

Morning? Mums, the flames... That voice? God's? Where?...

"EARL WRANGLER—NO, IT'S WILD MAN SKEEGOG FOR
PEARL AND EARL, LENORE AND SNORAM. HERE SHE
COMES, THAT NEW ONE CLIMBIN' THE WALL, HOTTEST
THING IN TOWN: *FRANNY'S FANNY*. STICK IT TO 'EM
SKEEGOG!"

Was that the dial? Good. So much for Skeegog. The *store*.
Up and at 'em, alright. Was there a brick on his head? Great
pressure, sheets of flame. Ethel, where was she? A note
pasted on the mirror, big black printing: "AWAY ON BUSINESS
FOR A FEW DAYS. REPORT TO MS. FARTLAR 9:00 AT
STORE." Half an hour to make it. Dress and run. Run and
dress. Out the door and—Futts at the elevator. Ease it shut
and wait...Someone yelling?...The radio, hadn't he turned?...

"YEAH, OH YEAH, AINT NUTTIN IN DUH WERLD, EWE

EEE AHH, LIKE DAT *FAH*-NEE..."

"Now for a brief newsbreak. Limited war has broken out in the East. And our hot spot of the hour: Flash Stud of Rolling Crud was arrested for possession of a controlled substance. More on the Crud situation as it develops."

Coast clear. Quickly to the elevator and—Mrs. Gribbley, walker emerging around her door, talking loudly.

"...*Stickle*, turn that blamed radio down. Can't hear to think! My Fred..."

Into the elevator, down and out. Volcanic sneezing, tingle of pepperoni fume.

"Geeshundheit, Horace, and many more."

"Mr. Joblobber..." Pipe fuming.

"Later, later, my good man. Here, Ripstrom, over here! I'll cab it too. Is Festin?...Hmm."

"FA LA LA LA *LA*, LA LA LA *LAH*. DRINK BREWBUSTERS AND LEARN WHAT LIFE CAN BE."

Not on a private street, not on Rostow! There it was though, its bottle-snout turning the corner. Did the driver have a Brewbuster in hand, give him the middle finger again? Maybe he'd be arrested for drunken driving or disturbing the peace. Not likely, not at all. Peace? There didn't seem to be any such thing. Well, of course—Mums...That was something else though, indeed it was.

*

"I understand, Miz Fartlar: I'm docked twenty-minutes for not punching in till now. You see at Company..."

She wasn't going to let him finish, mouth already moving. A tank, her hair bunned high, eyes of a drill instructor.

"Stickle, this is Store, not Company. At Store you follow Store rules. Miz Trench advises you're special case. Well, nobody 'special' here 'cept me and Miz Crump in the Cage. We manage Store, supervise, make rules you keep. Don't want beard on premises, stubble either. You'll see to that, *Stickle*: get the shave tomorrow, won't you? Cut the grass?"

"Yes, no time, I..."

"Apron is in back room over there with mop, cleanser, broom which you will use if customer breaks produce, jar, etcetera. Apron identifies you as clerk so customer knows where to direct the question. You will wear apron at all times in Store."

"Miz Fartlar..."

"No interruption. When truck comes in you stock aisles three, four, as printout here states. Stamp price with Stamper. Crump will *loan* you Stamper. If you lose or damage Stamper, that is deducted. Same with apron. You will also have responsibility for beer section. A space to be cleared for new product: Brewbuster. No drinking on job. Penalty: termination. See shoplifter: notify Mr. Snelly over there in beard and army boot. He's Store Detective. Catch you stealing, jail. Fill in form here, then proceed. Crump signals. Must go to Cage. Return form to Cage. You look familiar, Stickle. I never forget the face. Have you been in Store before, in trouble? I'll be checking."

"Perhaps you've seen me when—"

"Later, Stickle, I have no time."

"I understand. There is one question I must..."

Out of earshot. Strange way of talking: as if he were an illiterate. Maybe to save time, a shorthand of speech. That must be Miz Crump, head swiveling behind the glass partition, zooed in, roaming the stall. Was there straw in there, bran mash? Wrong attitude. Crump perhaps was more friendly. He had to get along with these people—at least try.

I never forget the face: Of course she'd seen him before—as a customer. Shopped there for years. Even given her or Crump hell once for not cashing a check. Zoos: Surely he was about to enter one. There was old lady Stringer ready to eyeball him, frown. Lucky he wasn't in uniform yet. Invisible bars, true, but he was inside, and they were out. Paranoid maybe, embarrassing beyond doubt.

"Phone, Stickle—a Doctor Foch. Calls are against policy for the worker unless they're emergency. Otherwise deduction. Take it here, at Cage."

"Thank you, Miz Crump."

"Deduction is from payroll."

"Doctor Foch?"

"Yes, Mr. Stickle. Heard you'd been assigned to the field, heh. Lucky fellah. Bring home the bacon on the sly. Eat for free. Some people just fall into it."

"I wouldn't quite say that Doctor—"

"Thing is, Mr. Stickle, you'll recall that spot Solly mapped on the old coconut? Could be sinus, an insect, defective circuit, even the tremors. Who knows? Maybe the old bulb is turning polka dot, rebelling, about to go *bink*. Yes yes. Ho. Whatever, we're straightening up records—year end and all that. Everything's to go on tape. Heard of Snatly and Broadspringer, the consultants?—driving us crazy."

"Yes, Futts is...Doctor Foch, you can't believe—"

"To finish, Mr. Stickle. You'll recall the appointment with Doctor Groat I had mentioned?—it's four-thirty this afternoon."

"Four-thirty? Well, my hours here last till—"

"Red alert, Mr. Stickle. Ciao."

"Miz Crump, you wanted?—"

"We've seen the face before, Stickle; Miz Fartlar, me. You have the look: maybe in the newspapers for crime. Worse. Best watch yourself. Keep the nose clean!"

"That's not true, Miz Crump, not at all."

A giraffish woman, rimless glasses: silver suns that blazed above.

"To leave at four-thirty, Stickle? First day? Shift runs till quarter to five."

"It's a doctor's appointment, Miz Crump, I must—"

"Deduction, fifteen minutes plus twenty already. Not good, eh, Stinkel, not—"

"It's Stickle, Hor—"

"Whatever. Store wants better. Otherwise it's *Downtown*. Look, red light! Truck's in. Shave Stinckly. You need the lawnmower. Rovel and you go to unloading. Truck is late. Red light still blinking. Hurry. No time to twiddle the thumbs."

*

"*Exercise*, my boy, a prescription for all seasons. Yes, oh my goodness, is it ever!"

"Nothing else, Doctor Groat, no *medicine*..." Was the man

competent? He resembled a small, white monkey. When he grinned—or was it more a grimace?—his lips curled back over chicklety teeth that gleamed and sparkled.

"Nothing for now, Mr. Stickle. A couple of reflexes were, ah, unusual. I'm suggesting to Doctor Foch that Solly give you another *whoop-dee-doo* in the New Year."

"But, Doctor Groat, will exercise really?—"

"To interrupt, Mr. Stickle. Like the song says: *It's Later Than you Think*. Your body, young fellah, is that of an eighty year old. Ashes to ashes, rust to dust. That's where you're headed unless drastic changes are made. Got sludge, toxic waste in your engine, old boy. Needs a tune-up. Strap Addidas on your doggies like I do. Peel rubber. I'm seventy-eight. Whatever the day, tremor or brownout, old Doc Groat blitzes the track every day. Run in marathons, swim laps alternate afternoons. Sports?: Every game is my game. Honorary member of the Billy Goats. Fit as a fiddle. Feel ten years old. Have the love life of a rabbit. Yes indeedy, puts lead in the old pencil, it surely does. Give this to nurse, if you will."

"But, Doctor Groat, how much exercise? When?..."

"Sorry, Mr. Stickle, blinking red. Next appointment due. Read *Man of Steel* by Granger Stonewall. Tells you everything. Now—ah, Mrs. Gribbley. And how are we today?"

"Terrible, I—Stickle, you look awful. Pea soup in the pot ten years later."

"Hello, Mrs. Gribbley. I...toe, your walker... *Get your blasted*..."

"Sorry about that, Stickle. Shouldn't get your feet in the way."

"My bunion, it's on my bunion! Pull the damn thing up! Yank it!..."

"Don't swear at me, you wretched man. My Fred never swore in his whole life, never drank. A saint he was."

" *Off,* Mrs. Gribbley. Goddammit off!"

Ah hell, she was digging it in to get leverage. There, finally. But now the agony increased, shivered up his body, screamed behind his eyes.

"Doctor Groat?..."

He didn't hear, leading Gribbley to another room chortling, chattering. Had he pinched her seat? Impossible, but she was

61

giggling, now both cackling. "Doctor Groat, are there any vitamins, medicines?..."

"You still here? I told you, Mr. Stickle, run for your life or the devil will get you. Heh."

"My Fred did it, Doctor Groat, every day for thirty years. Died on the thirtieth lap over at Gimpers Park at fifty-five. Healthiest man you'd ever want to meet. Doctor, where?..."

"In the stirrups, Mrs. Gribbley, you know, like before."

"Will it tickle, same's last time?"

"Mr. Stickle, you can give me that."

"Pardon, Nurse, what?..."

"The bill, Mr. Stickle, the paper in your hand."

"Oh, of course, sorry."

Stirrups, couldn't be?...What a horrible thought.

"Did you hear me, Mr. Stickle?"

"Yes—no...Nurse, I was thinking..."

"Fifty dollars, your bill is *fifty* dollars."

"Fifty...Let's see, I only have ten in cash. Doesn't Amalgamated pick up the bill? Doctor Foch referred..."

"Mr. Stickle, practically everything here is cash. I've never heard of Doctor Foch or this Amalgamated whatever."

"That's odd. May I phone Doctor Foch?..."

Damn, it was after five. Foch would have left. Nurse seemed angry, punching a button. Was that steam on her thick glasses? Throat pulsing, a bullfrog tensing before the leap. Nasty thoughts. Why the distortions, viciousness in his perceptions recently?

That squat woman who'd just flung open the glass doors to the office seemed familiar. Hard to see the face though, the purple beret pulled low. Yet there was something about her...

"Miz Fartlar, isn't it? Gout, I believe."

"Yes Nurse. Just came from Store and..."

"Stickle, it's *Stickle* isn't it?"

"Yes, Miz Fartlar, I..."

"Forgot the *punchout*, Stickle. Must punch in *and* punch out. No punch out, no pay for the day. Payroll is done by computer. Card needs the hole. No holes, no pay."

"How did you know I didn't?..."

"Saw you leave, didn't punch out."

"I...why didn't you tell?...Nurse, here, I have Master Charge.

That will have to do."

"We don't usually...Let me check."

"I can assure you, Nurse..."

Blasted woman *would* have to confirm its validity. Mist crisscrossed her bifocals. Fartlar was staring at him, never blinking, sucking something between her teeth. Nurse on the phone, frowning.

"I see. The number has a hold on it! *Stolen* you say? Thank you."

"Mr. Stickle you are in possession of a stolen credit card, a criminal offense."

"Knew I'd seen you before, Stickle: Post Office—wanted."

"I'm not wanted, Miz Fartlar, *anywhere*."

"Nurse, will you please give me the phone, my card? Thank you...

"Hello, I am inquiring about Number 4290 001 047 722. Right. Yes, just a moment ago. You tapped into the *wrong* system? Would you repeat that information again? Nurse, listen please."

"Let's you off the hook, Mr. Stickle. Can't be too careful, though. You're not a regular."

"Don't forget, Stickle: Store, eight sharp tomorrow. Not a weekend. No slugabedding. Don't punch in—deduction."

The cold air numbed his head, slowed the racers in his veins. *No pay for the day*. Was that what Fartlar had said? Perhaps a poetry of Store—hidden meanings, value. More than could be said for the doctor's wisdom offered at fifty dollars a shot.

Exercise? Ethel had offered the same advice free over the last few years. Jog, run—what was the matter with walking? He'd walk home, pass Gimpers Park. They ran or jogged on the track year round. Hadn't been over there in years. Maybe he'd go once around the grounds—halfway was plenty. Forget it, tomorrow was soon enough. A drink, that was the prescription of Doctor Stickle: a large one, immediately. The Hammer's Claw up ahead winked an invitation: "For All You Ever Wanted Out Of Life, And More—Brewbuster." The bartender speaking, looming close, mustache a darkening frown that curled downwards disappearing into beard and mouth.

"Mister?"

"Hello...Vodka, please."

Beer seemed the popular drink. Why did he feel so...so odd, embarrassed, in these places? The Claw was Store, Store for men, workingmen: dirt on the boots, big wrists, the hearty curse. He lacked insignia—his suit and tie, the wrong badge. Or maybe it was something else, a feeling he didn't belong, not in their world, not in Futts's world either for that matter.

"For the Bulls or Crashers, Jack?"

"Pardon?"

The huge man's cap read *RAM*. A dragon—or was it a werewolf?—glared from the back of his hand.

"Who?...Crashers, I guess...That league, I don't..."

"Crashers! Strunk, wimp here is Crashers."

"Sorry, Mister, this is a Bull's only party. Can't serve yuh. It's Bowl, the final. Try Bubbas Package across the street."

"I understand. Tell that...that tattoo beside me I have a black belt in karate, was a captain...Yes, *you*. I deal in chimneys, smoke rings. Bodies in bathtubs. Phssh. Careful, you could slip, end up like Chicken Little. Goodnight."

Trembling, head quivering. Disgusted with himself. The rage (or just plain stupidity?) had surfaced again. RAM was probably drunk, had a blip on *his* coconut. And himself?: out of control, desiring what?—revenge for other things, a taste of blood? What if Tattoo had attacked him? Lucky only his mouth had opened and shut several times. Bubbas—that sign blinking at the corner? A half pint? No, a pint was in order. Sit on a bench, pull himself together, have a few nips.

*

How long had he been there? Was that his bottle beside him, empty? Hands, a numbness...Gloves?...There, at his feet, buried, whitened paws, unmoving in the snow. The night, its blackness, sifting gold—*splinkers* to Karaki: light still reaching, travelling on in endless search.

Was Ethel with the human ax, splitting logs, smashing rocks? Or were they?...Hard to imagine. Would Ethel?...could there be steps and strokes for that too?—belts for advanced technique?

Manny's Computerized Dating: All You Ever Wanted In A Mate And More. Did the flashing neon spell that message up ahead? Colors zigzagged, winked and streaked in mottled blur before the sign cleared again. Should he?…All he wanted was someone to talk to, connect with: a regular person, an old fashioned *she.*

Corny?—perhaps. But computers and all the modern stuff were *itzes*: "Make *it* talk, roll over." Wasn't that what Futts had said? Yet hadn't most mechanical things in the past been *shes*?: ships, cars, planes—like women in other days: obedient, responsive to throttle or pedal, switch. The *itzes,* though, were like the new ladies: incomprehensive, whirling on strange energies, convertible entities.

To ask for something—no somebody—familiar, did that make him unusual, subject to penalty? No matter, it was all he wanted right now, and more.

*

Was he in the foyer of the Battle Arms? How had he gotten there?: the homing instinct?

What had the sleek young man in Manny's said after directing him to punch out small slots opposite questions on a card?: "Sir would perhaps like to deposit his offering in Mate Matcher?" Had the machine resembled a woman?: a reddish tongue flicking out to receive his application? The clerk had grinned, thumb and forefinger shaping a donut which he'd waved happily, his face a chalky moon rising beneath a mass of hair, a gleaming dark swept up and back. Something sleazy about it all. Why then did he feel a tingle of excitement?: the prospect of checking back in a couple of days for a date?: maybe the two tapes he'd bought for the video cassette recorder? —Virgin Virginia's First Nite and Strange Shirly's Secret. What had the man said?: that the girls on those particular tapes talked directly to a *Henry*, the closest he could come to a *Horace.* It seemed a dream, but for the package in his hands.

"That you, Stickle?"

65

"Who?..." The intercom. Must've had his finger on a buzzer.

"Gribbley here. Don't play games, Stickle. I know yer voice. I'll get the law. It'll be jail, no key. Never did like your mother-in-law, did yuh? My Fred, he adored Mother Gribbley. She and Grand Mums, they lived with us for years. Why..."

"The little dog laughed to see such a sight, and I jumped over the moon. God bless, Mrs. Gribbley; God bless Fred too, and to all a good night."

"Don't try to smart talk me, Stickle, I'll..."

Wonderful. By lifting his finger she was gone. Magic. Someone coming.

"Mr. Futts, good evening. Seem to have forgotten my key, could you?..."

"Key to life is *time*, Stickle. Opens every lock."

"I see. What locks, Mr. Futts?"

"Time-locks, all combinations. Class in half hour. Hurry Stickle, attendance counts. No attendance, black mark. Five, no job, pauper's grave. Simple as *yes* and *no*. A sobering thought, is it not?"

"Class?...No one told..."

Futts already scurrying inside with his mail, the door clicking shut before he could follow. Maybe Snoley the janitor would...holding his key all the time. What he needed now was warmth, food—something more substantial than peanuts or apples. Time for those snacks later. Maybe too much, likely too little.

*

"Pig-Out? Another...I mean a Whammo and Monster. Six pack of beer. Pardon? Only Brewbuster? No—well yes, that'll do. Eleven sixty-six Rostow, Battle Arms Apartments. Horace—Mr. Stickle. Thank you."

Damn, nothing in the frig to munch. A world of negatives: no this, out of that, sold. Maybe the cupboard. There, way in the back—gin. No doubt the reason why Mum and Ethel seemed so—what?: sly, bouncy at times. Half a quart too. He'd put on Virgin Virginia and have a drink, wait for Pig-Out. Hmmm, the tape was in color.

There came Virginia, so tall, blonde—a movie queen, his

66

very own. Husky voice, eyes lowered. Shy, waiting to be coaxed.

"Hello Henry, I'm Virginia. Do you like me? I hope so. I find you terribly attractive."

"Thank you. I...I've never..." Never what? Talked to an image, a flickering phantom? *I can relate to human beings, not graphs of them on screens.* He'd said that to Futts, hadn't he? But this was different. Virginia, slim and creamy, looked so...so attractive, available, sitting on a couch, *his* couch, low neckline on the black dress, high heels, one shoe half off as she wiggled her foot.

"Do you think I'm pretty, Henry? People tell me I have nice legs. See?"

"I'm sure, oh yes, oh my, they are..."

The dress suddenly sliding to her thighs. A garter?...could that be?...A drink, he needed...

"Have a cocktail, Henry. Think I'll mix one too. Get into something more comfortable."

Standing now, tall, erect, hint of a sway to her walk. Smiling at him over her shoulder, tossing the waist-length hair. Yes, a drink while she changed, that sounded good.

Coming back already? No, just her face around the doorway of the bedroom, eyes huge, so shy...peeking...

"Ready or not Henry..."

"*Telegram* for Mr. Stickle."

"What!"

"Mr. Stickle there? *Telegram.*"

"Yes yes, coming. Where is?..."

"Flat on the floor, not a sound!"

"Who?..."

The man filled the doorway, fedora low, gun a toy in his fist. Whiff of zoo, disinfectant.

"Where is it, Stickle? Guzman says..."

"Drop it, Zalt, *now!*"

"Are you all right, Mr. Stickle?"

"Yes, who?..." A tubby man, shiny bald.

"Detective Fasten, Detective Lieutenant Henry Fasten.

"Against the wall, Zalt."

"Henry, do you like me better this way? I'll do anything you..."

"What?...Ahh, I see, Stickle, you're one of those—"

"Watch out!..."

Too late. The gun flew from Fasten's hand. A flurry of movement and Zalt disappeared with lizard speed. Shouting from the hallway. His Monster and Whammo splattered over wall and floor. An elderly man thrashing face down in the mess. Fasten on one knee wringing his hand, pate aflame, voice choked.

"Blasted filth of yours to blame, Stickle. Diverted my attention. Hand broke, Zalt free. Should arrest *you*. Won't be long. We've been watching, listening: Infinity Beepers, total surveillance. Closing in. You're corralled. Guzman's playing games. If Zalt or I don't nail you, the others will."

"Henry, your hair, I'd love to run my fingers..."

"Detective Fasten, what are you talking?—"

"Silence, I want to see...If this is porno, I'll have the store closed, shuttered..."

"Oh Henry, whisper you love me, tell me you'll do anything..."

"Pig-Out for Stickle. You Stickle? Delivery's ruined. Twelve dollars. You owe, all of it. Not my fault. Should sue you people. Back's jammed again, crippled..."

"Here's fifteen. I'm sorry there wasn't anything I could do to stop—"

"*Sorry* won't fix my back. *Sorry's* no good."

"Another fight, eh Stickle? Brawlin', drinkin', killin'. Your day is comin'. My Fred in his whole life never lifted a hand..."

"I'm sure he didn't, Mrs. Gribbley."

"I'll be in touch, Stickle. Wouldn't go too far away." Trafficking's fifteen years *flat*. No parole."

"But Mr....Detective Fas..."

Hurrying to the elevator, not listening. Gribbley approaching, peering over his shoulder into the apartment.

"Luther, my love, what ecstasy. I knew you'd come..."

"An abomination unto the Lord, Stickle. She's almost nikkid, and he's taking off his..."

"Fred would love it, I'm sure, Mrs. Gribbley. Have a nice evening. Goodnight."

Luther. That gigolo with pipe and ascot, belching voice. There wasn't supposed to be another man. Now a close up of Luther's slippers...

"Virginia, my dear, you look ravishing. Let me..."

68

"What would Henry say, Luther? After all?..."

"Henry's a wimp, my dear, a perfect mouse. Over here, love, where I can see..."

That did it. Off with the video. What the?...still on. Button stuck or...Luther adjusting his dressing gown, grinning, the pipe being tamped, lit, clouds of smoke becoming script: "Part One Of Virginia And Henry At Home. Part Two Available At All Adult Bookstores And Novelty Shops. The End." Finally a blank screen. Not quite: the faint image of a face— his reflection? No, not his, Luther's: hand extended, middle finger raised. An afterglow, seeing things?

Stomach growling, head reeling. Food, anything...By the door a piece of Whammo, pepperoni glistening on his shoe. The TV crackling, picture sideways, blurred, now upside down. A blast of static, then the voice, a roaring in his ears that cried:

"God loves you! Do you hear me, sinners, He loves you! Every last rotten soul."

A man in a red beanie and black cape glared from the screen, swirled his robe, balled his fists and shook them violently. "It says so right here. Do you love *Him*? Show your love, mail twenty-five dollars..."

Had to be something better.

"Killer bees, Bruce darling. Get in the truck..."

"I was given three weeks to live. It's now been four, Martha. Maybe God listened to my prayers, will heal..."

"Shut up Fred. What does it matter? You're not a...a *man* anymore. Do you understand me, Fred? Leave me alone. Can't you see The Numpers are on? It's *Part Two*."

Would Ethel speak to him that way some day?

"I vant your blood, dahling, all of it, *now*..."

The creature resembled Priddle. One more try.

"We're going in Bruno, left wing on fire, too low to bail out. Let's take the rotten bastards with us."

More like it. Felt a bit that way too, except it was hard to know who the enemy was. What a fireball. Ship a sheet of flame, the plane a crimson torch. Done in a pond or swimming pool, though. All a farce: just make believe with firecrackers and miniatures. Would it were the same at Company: a joke, the cry of April Fool.

The room was turning slowly, a carousel about to whirl with...Shadows, faces, crowding, staring at the window, mouths agape. Fartlar, Groat, and there was Crump. Now Priddle, Futts—Gribbley too. Fingers pointing, wagging; babble rising to a moan: "No pay today, no job, hooray, hoor..."

"*No!*"

Had he yelled? Must've fallen asleep on the floor. He'd been alive under glass in the coffin as it coasted rapidly toward arching fires ahead. Men, with visored faces, torches, leather suits, had lined the rails on which he rolled. "No pay we say, no way no way," had come the chant while music blared and dancers swirled. He'd been lifted, floated, on a silvered cloud, then looking down had seen the man in red and midnight gown about to drop his cinders in a chamber pot.

"Going in, going in, oh Lord amen," a voice had wailed, now an endless belling in his head.

He'd adjust the radio to FM; classical music would soothe him to sleep.

"EARL WRANGLER HERE, FOR ALL THE FOLKS OUT THERE AT PIG-OUTS ACROSS THE LAND: *I'M JUST HOG WILD OVER—*"

"We interrupt regular programming for this brief newsbreak. It is believed war in the East has spread.

"Now our special for the hour: Flash Stud of Crud has been released. Details as they happen.

"We return you again to classical favorites for lovers only."

Later, jerked awake, he'd reached for Virginia glowing palely beside him, only to find Miz Fartlar in his grasp—or was it Crump? Asleep, awake, so hard to tell. In bubbling lava there was Mums, a spire of flame with blackened finger speared at him. Finger?—no!: Karaki, darkened arrow streaking in with handcuffs glistening, dangling from his teeth.

"I didn't do it; not me, not me!"

It didn't help; the blindfold placed.

"Ready, aim, *deduction*," barked the voice.

And for a little while he thought he slept.

8

DID I NOT tell you, Stickle, clerks shave the whisker? Face has more bush today. Unacceptable. This is Store, not slum."

"Sorry, Miz Fartlar, forgot. Last night, no food, Pig-Out, I..."

Gin tickled his nose, still a bit high. No breakfast again. Teeth impacted with slivers of pepperoni, odds and ends of Monster.

"Pig? You have the pig, Stickle? Explains smell — stockyard. Reasonable odor is required by Store. One more chance. Third strike — out, downtown. Those two men know you, Stickle? Tall one, he waves over here."

"I don't believe... Yes, it's Mr. Joblobber and Futts, they're doing a survey—"

"Peddlers not allowed."

"Mr. Stickle, you're looking chirper. Must be the exercise. Wonderful day, good to be alive. Excuse, continue with your customer and..."

"Not customer, supervisor. Crump and me, *supervisors*. Stickle here will answer the question. Have business at Cage with Crump."

"Let me introduce myself, Miss..."

"*Miz* Fartlar."

"I'm Bob Joblobber and this is Ripstrom Futts. Now, Wench..."

"Not to call me wench! Never to use that—"

"No no, Miz Fartlar: WENCH. It's the robot. WEN is short for Wendy. The C.H. stands for *Consumers' Helper.* Now—"

"*Robot?* These people friends of yours, Stickle? Playin' the game. Out from the Home for a day. I'm busy—"

"The name is Futts, Miz Fartlar. Let me sum up quickly. As Joblobber began to tell you, we're doing a management survey for headquarters—Snatly, Broadspringer. R & D at Amalgamated has devised Wench to assume Produce Engineer Grades One, Two, Three, Four functions. The whole store, all Amalgamated stores in time, will likely become totally robotized, computerized, automated. The pilot project will run for a week or more."

"Miz Fartlar, please excuse Ripstrom's brusqueness. Heavy schedule: meetings, reports—"

"Store run completely by machine? What is this Snoty and whatever? Must be crazy. How can customer talk to machine? What happens to me, Crump?"

"Retraining, perhaps a second act in your life: nursing, movies, the stage, running a boutique. A cat has nine lives, Miz Fartlar, but for us who knows: one, ten, a million? The choice is ours, isn't it? Of course, indeedy do. Now—"

"The *Nurse,* bedpan! Old men, hoses! I wouldn't—"

"Ah, Miss Fartlar, I know you're excited. Marvelous possibilities. But to finish: Wench will be set up later this afternoon, go into operation tomorrow with technicians to monitor and assist. You might pass this on to Miz Crump. Let me get to you Mr.—"

"*Excited. Possibility.* I tell you—"

"Wonderful, Miz Fartlar, I'm glad you agree. Now Mr. Stickle, your interests have been carefully considered also, an alternate plan arranged. In fact, Miz Fartlar, I believe he was picked up at noon on Headquarters' payroll. We'll check on—"

"Not to listen to the gibberish any longer. Punch out, Stickle. No punch out, no—"

"Miz Fartlar, I forgot again—the punch in, I mean..."

"No pay today, no pay yesterday. Nothing plus nothing— figure it out, Stickle: goose egg. Crump gives the signal. Must go now."

"Fine Miz Fartlar, give her the good news. We'll talk later. Now, Mr. Stickle, this is the idea: Miz Mawsley and Trench before they left on a field trip agreed you could take Ramon's place on the Executive floor."

"*Executive floor,* Mr. Joblobber?"

Had his expertise, experience, value to Company finally been recognized? What was the saying?: "All comes to he who waits." He'd sat in the shadows for almost a lifetime, and now his name had been called, the reward upon him.

"Yes, executive floor. Ramon apparently replaced Hang- linger a few months ago when he retired."

"Hanglinger, old Hangy, the *coffee cart man?*"

"That's the Hanglinger, Mr. Stickle. You'll take over during Ramon's convalescence. Continue on the payroll, preserve employment benefits while you qualify under the retraining program. The job requires punctuality. You will serve coffee, soda; keep the Danish warm and related functions. The gods are smiling on you, Mr. Stickle. Lucky sevens, box cars. Can't ask for more, can we?

"You had something to add, Ripstrom?"

"Out-house instruction commenced last night, Stickle. Record shows *absent.* Black mark. Check with Mr. Priddle. Festin's on roll. Technology waits on no man. Management won't play checkers with you forever. Careful, or you'll be skipped, taken off the board."

"Quite right, Ripstrom. But Mr. Stickle is a survivor: the mouse that swims; a weed upon a barren rock. Keep up the good work. Enjoy. Make it a good one. Must be off. Oh yes, the rest of the day's yours, Horace. Start tomorrow. Happy holiday. Ciao."

"Mr. Joblobber, where do I report?...who?..."

Waving to him, a half salute. Calling out something, ruddy face beaming as he rounded the aisle.

An iron grip on his arm.

"Apron, Stickle, Stamper too! Not to be taken from premises. Rip in apron, I see. A minus."

"You didn't need to grab me that way, Miz Fartlar, I would have remembered."

"Hah, halfway to the door. *Remember,* he says. Probly steal the grocery wagons too. Snelly says he seen you before. He never forgets the face."

"Quite right, Miz Fartlar, I've been a customer here for years. But I may never come back. You may never see my face again."

"Don't you dare smart talk me, Stickle, I won't—"

"Miz Fartlar, my name is Horace, Mr. Stickle. One or the other. That's not much to ask, is it?"

Her face a riot of color, pushing past him, signaling Crump. Perhaps he'd been rude, but then one had to try and retain some dignity, just a bit. He'd pick up eggs, a loaf of bread. Without a bite to eat and soon, he most surely would be skipped, absent forever. The ultimate in black stigmata.

Why not walk past Gimpers Park on the way home? Maybe Groat was right: jog, exercise—get his engine shipshape. Could do the trick. New motor, better mileage. Might be just the thing to help him go the distance. Jock stuff though. Never had been much good at athletics in school.

What had been his high school gym teacher's name?: ah yes, Raglov Strang, Bulldog Strang with the steel wool hair. Always picking on him and Frawley and a few others. Given him failing grades consistently. Addressed the class at the last session and told them the only failures were those who didn't go *flat out.*

"Sixty, if I'm a day," he'd yelled. "A double somersault on the trampoline. By gar, I'll do or die."

He'd gone flat out, alright, short legs propelling him toward the ceiling where he'd tucked into the flip. But his heart had failed him badly. Would he ever forget Strang hurtling downward, landing with his head caught between the springs, eyes bulging, mouth an oval of surprise. *Flat out:* There was a...a kind of purity about the idea: shooting stars, sails touching foam. Something he'd never known, likely never would.

Was Strang right, that failures lacked drive?: didn't become fireballs of energy equivalent to their weight, as Futts would have it? Was that the self-fulfillment so many talked about? Something bothersome about that idea. Intention, feeling, didn't they count, have to be tied into the whole thing? Yet it was hard to know what was really worth the effort, or how to make it.

There was Gimpers ahead. Joggers three abreast, grim, the columns stretching to the curve and out of sight. That stout man breaking rank, shaking his head—was he crying *no more, no more*? By the bench, someone on the grass rolling from side-to-side, gasping.

"Are you alright? I just wondered, is there anything?..."

"Shhhh...thank you...lost breath...better soon...wonderful ...later...try again..."

"To the *right*, the *right*!"

"What?..."

A gust of wind, boots pounding past. "*Left*, to the *left*!" A spray of gravel at his feet. Another body bearing down, face contorted, writhing lips. And up ahead, a rack of bars where people hung suspended upside down in metal boots. That white-haired man, was he alright?: his face a purpling crimson mask as back-and-forth he swung, eyes closed.

Behind him now the flash of lights and siren's wail. The man approaching might know...

"Excuse me..."

"Can't stop. Heel toe, heel toe, cut cut, heel..." Arms sawing, turkey strut, the cadence an explosive shout.

An outstretched figure by the ambulance, the medic thumping on his chest. Even so, the crowd churned by without stop or break in stride. Beside him running on the spot, a cadaverous chap gasping.

"Cranly...the man down. Round twenty times, I think. Myself...notched ten...But gotta stitch—godawful pain...a ruptured—"

"Will he?...alright?..."

A vein in the jogger's head beat furiously. There was a ring of tubing around his waist.

"Don't know. Happens to old Cran every once in a while. Pushes too hard, a 'gung ho' man. Am too, myself—sometimes. Not in Cran's league, though."

"Why? I mean, crazy isn't it?"

"Crazy?—*Cran*?"

"Twenty, why'd he do it twenty times? He could kill—"

"To get fit, increase aerobic capacity, live longer, perhaps forever. Anybody'd know that. For Cran—*Cranners*—it's religion, philosophy, a spiritual perfecting you can see in the mirror...count in laps or a time-clock. What do you mean, *why*? Everyone knows. Christ promised eternal life. This is the first step. The ultimate therapy."

"But..."

Better not bother the man anymore. The burst of speech had brought spittle to his lips, sobs as he continued to run in place. Face swollen, sweat cascading from his forehead, streaming over rimless glasses, he appeared on the verge of collapse. Cranly, pudgy, ashen, was mumbling on the stretcher being hustled to the ambulance. A great cheer rose from others jogging in small circles around the scene. The man beside him was speaking again, shouting.

"Cran said twenty-one or die! What a guy! More like him, and we could take the world with one arm! Makes you proud to be one of us. Think I'll lap it once more for old Cran. Ciao."

Who was that bearing down on him now, pointing, yelling?— Priddle!

"*Mare*ee Christmas, Stickle. Better ask Santa for some jogging togs, old boy. Running shoes are the thing, you know. Not those cement mixers you're wearing. Get angel wings, Flyers like mine. Hundred bucks. Worth every penny. *Deerfoot*, they call me. Start pedaling if I were you. Might improve your image, influence decisions. Futts and Joblobber aren't far behind. Fitness buffs. Enjoy."

Hadn't he called joggers *sneaker-freaks* a while back? And now he was *Deerfoot*.

"Look Priddle, that black mark for absent. I didn't know classes..." Not listening. Careening off, a candycane in maroon and white, purple coonskin jammed over his ears.

Evening already? Yes, streetlights flaring across the park. The twosome at the curve—Futts and Joblobber. He'd ask about retraining, where instruction was...

Airborn, flying, groceries gone, then a bush cushioning his fall. Dammit, logs spaced on the track which people *jumped*

76

jumped jumped like kangaroos. Here came Futts, a human hovercraft in black. Now Joblobber, waving, shouting, leaping in fluid arcs.

"Next time, Mr. Stickle, better luck next time. Connect, we must connect. We're not just ships, vessels passing in the dark. Racers all Horace, we're runners of life. Grand, oh it surely is!"

"I...tripped, wasn't really looking..."

Already past him, joined with Priddle at the next pit. The three now in unison: arms windmilling, legs flying in alternate directions. Had Priddle pointed over his shoulder? Could have sworn his middle finger went up as the threesome moved off.

Why was it elephants and tortoises lived to a ripe old age and moved very slowly, while flies and rabbits zipped around and died after a few years or weeks? Runners everywhere in packs hording oxygen, whooshing out clouds of carbon dioxide. One could be gassed if trapped by such traffic. Not for him. He'd walk, if anything, to the frig, bed, bus stop; perhaps wander round Gimpers on a nice day.

Jogging could lead to worse things than sailing into a bush. What of stroke, paralysis?: a nurse Fartlar barreling his wheelchair down freeways, bashing it into produce towering above him in food stores, and finally, outraged at his uselessness, hurling it together with his withered body into a chasm, the echoes of her triumphant bellow reverberating from the cliffs? —*Deduction, one Stickle*—over and over until finally the exploding whiteness caught him up, revealing Mum Granger winging his way, flanked by God and Satan, their verdict a thunder rumbling into eternity: *Guilty as charged.* The sentence?: that he *forever and ever punch in, punch out. Hell on weekdays, weekends Upstairs, if no black mark.*

Indeed, running could be bad medicine. For the present, it was more than enough that his shaky legs carry him home.

*

Someone had obviously been in the apartment. Yes, one could make that assumption: sofas, chairs, mattresses slashed in various interesting patterns. Lamps, tables, dressers

77

overturned. Everything was very messed up. All in all it gave the place a lived-in feeling. A home that reflected his mind. *YOUR NEXT* advised the message scrawled on the hall mirror. Another deduction of some kind, no doubt.

Were there people, things—a force—that sought his scalp, the spirit of Mum Granger in hot pursuit? Depended likely on the connections made: too many and you were paranoid, too few and one wandered the labyrinth. The gunman and Fasten had mentioned Guzman. Plus there'd been the detective's comment about trafficking and fifteen years: a deduction for certain he couldn't face. Better contact Fasten and get more information, report the break-in.

"Central Administration? A Detective Fasten please. What? Yes, I'll hold."

"Hello, this is Horace Stickle. I'm at home and the whole apartment...*Stickle,* Horace Stickle. It's about last night. You'd mentioned Guzman and I..."

"No, I'm not stuck. It's *Stickle.* I can't hear very...Circuits jamming...I see...Who is this?"

"What hotline? No, I don't want to contribute. Will you please—"

"*Jackpot?* I want Detective Fasten. They've threatened to kill..."

"Suicide what? No, *them,* not *me.* I don't want to kill...not myself..."

"Who?...Detective Karaki?"

"I haven't any confession to...Hello, I want..."

"*Information?* Please connect me with..."

"Just information? No connections? Who is?..."

"Operator? I want Central Admin—I just *had* information, they transferred... *Hello,* can you please?...A recorded announcement?..."

Damn, now what?...Disconnected?—no dead. Deceased, the line had expired. Not even breathing a dial tone—suffocated, no doubt. Jammed, overloaded—Towers of Babel become malignant, electronic cancers strangling communication, attacking sanity, infecting the brain. Was this to be the amazing result of new technologies?: endless hives of information breeding upon themselves; floods of data that would drown meaning in fact, raise confusion to a science.

Would the so-called revolution Joblobber promised cause people to become second class citizens of the heart? Data mongers? Passionless eunuchs making love to flickering screens? Could the new elites deal with those apples? Better still, was he able to boil an egg, the only one intact from his Gimpers tumble? Didn't matter. The lights were gone, apartment dark.

Branches of the tree through the picture window were spiders racing on the moon, skeletons that waved and danced. They seemed to beckon, grin, then leap away: an offer made and then withdrawn. The story of his life it seemed.

Yet luck could change, couldn't it? You had to believe that, somehow trust it would. Better still, *make* it change. But was that putting the cart before the Stickle, or the Danish before the coffee? He'd soon find out, perhaps too soon.

9

"GOOD MORNING, I'm Horace...Mr. Stickle. Mr...Ramon's job...while he's in the hospital. I...the coffee cart, Danish... keep it hot. I believe they said..."

Once again it was first grade. Miss Brome behind her desk, hair bunned, glasses glinting, eyes accusing. Even now he needed a pee.

"Mr. Echewy disappeared last night. Came through on my screen a few minutes ago. There he goes again. Miss Cuddy will instruct as to Mr. Moloch's service. Through the door over there. Mr. Stoneball will be in later. Service for the Chairman is to be in ten minutes. Mr. Schwingalt is in attendance. We're on hold. Quickly, Mr. Stickle. Mr. Echewy was always punctual. Inconvenient to go at a time like this."

"Yes, thank you, I..."

Could the stunning blonde in the next office be Miss Cuddy? So much like Virgin Virginia. Smiling, nodding to him as she answered the phone.

"Washington, Secretary Blight? Mr. Moloch? Right away. Could I help?..."

"Miss Cuddy?..."

"Yes, is there something?…"

"I'm Stickle, Mr…Horace…The cart—coffee. I'm supposed…"

"Quickly, Mr. Stickle. The pantry, those sliding doors. Hurry, please. Mr. Moloch is running late. We're on standby."

Was that the cart?: a gleaming cylinder, panel of buttons at one end? Where was the coffee? Hadn't Futts mentioned buns, Danish? No food anywhere. Burnished vats, a rack of carving knives.

Three buzzes. Must be the intercom on the wall with the switch underneath. Flip it up and…Voices, men's. He must have connected with Moloch's office.

"…Yes, Mr. Secretary. President Ralpher? Visit, *here*? Premier Gorshev too? Of course we run a tight ship. Most up-to-date technology, operations systems. Be glad to show…A great honor for Amalgamated…

"*Miss Cuddy*, we've been cut off! Would you?…It's Treasury, Schwingalt. Your friend Blight. You heard?: a gift, blessing. The event, publicity, could make the stock rise, our options could be exercised. God knows, we could use—*Miss Cuddy*, will you reconnect?…"

Two more buzzes. Maybe for him this time. "Miss Cuddy?"

"Mr. Stickle, you're to serve now. Don't forget the uniform."

"Uniform? Miss Cuddy, I don't have?…Ramon didn't give…"

"He may be dead, Mr. Stickle. He's off screen. Hurry. Red light's on."

"But the coffee, where is it? I can't find…"

"Black, Mr. Moloch always has his black. I must go. Quickly, we're *all* on standby now."

Should he just leave, forget it? Uniform? There, on the hanger behind the door. Big, the white suitcoat almost to his knees. Pants far too long. Use his own. Move the cart, shove harder. Something stuck. Footsteps.

"Troubles? Stoneball's the name. It's on *lock*."

"Pardon…Ramon was…I…"

"Chewy's gone. Lever six locks the wheels. Roll on four red—that button. Tilts, needs new coasters. Chef, I'm…The bell, hear that. Time. Must cook."

"Coffee? Where? I haven't seen…"

Stoneball in white resembled a snowman, except for the

nose, a button of crosshatched red.

"In the cannister. Heat on eleven. There you go...*watch* ..."

"I can't hold..."

The wagon was pulling him down a slight incline toward swinging doors which suddenly flew outwards to Moloch's office. The cart stopped on the plush rug. Several cups had fallen. Damn, he'd walked over two with a crunch. Smoke, he smelled...

"What is this? Who are you?"

"I'm Horace...Mr. Ramon, I mean Chewy, Echewy..."

"I'm Mr. Moloch, not Echewy. To repeat, what *is* this?..."

"Mr. Moloch, Mr. Ripstrom and Futts were responsible...My wife, Miz Tren—Mawsley arranged it."

Why wouldn't the cart budge? If he could only move to the desk where the two men were sitting, things might go easier.

Moloch unsettled him: a bald Lincoln with something wrong about the eyes: darting, sly roaches under beetle brows—a giant insect peering at him while grabbing for the phone.

"Miss Cuddy, who is this man on tumbril? Where is Ramon? *Lost,* you say? Then Stoneball?...Men's room...No I don't want...Miss Cuddy, the *President*... We've been disconnec... You there, Mr....whatever, we'll take service at the desk."

"Yes, Mr. Moloch. Very sorry about all this, I..."

Had the lever stuck? No, it was up. The wheels, back ones crooked. A sharp kick...There, deep breath and *shove* ...moving...skidding sideways. Pull back harder, almost... Hands slippery, losing grip...A wisp of smoke and coffee dribbling on the rug—chocolate fingers curling round a fallen Danish ringed with flame.

Blasted machine, if only...The coffee *would* be served. Foot stuck. Bend down and...his head, a pain, then crimson flashed behind his eyes as someone entered sweeping past—no, stopping, touching, hand on arm. A woman, gaunt, a spire above him rising, talking...

"...Accident, a grease spot here, loose wire there. No guarantees, my good man, never. Now Maddox, I must have a word—"

"I've *told* you, there's no need to visit—"

"I don't believe we've met, Mr?..."

"Schwingalt. Was just on my way out."

"Schwing—Jerry, this is my wife, Grunulda. Look dear, can't this wait? The President—"

"Just to remind you of the Tilversmiths—Harbor View, darling, the Revolution Room. Remember, the one that spins. I *know* you'll be able to make it. They're friends, *my* friends."

"Look, there is no way with all—"

"Tonight Maddox, eight o'clock. Where there's a will…For heaven sakes help that man with the coffee service!"

"It's all right, I've…there…"

Still wouldn't budge. Shove harder, lift and push and…Tilting, spilling…foot trapped, burning…

"My desk! Look what you've!…Over everything. My pants are!…"

"Your red button, dear, the phone."

"Get this god…mess…Tell whoever it is, Miss Cuddy, I cannot…*Him?* Yes, I'll…Give me two minutes… *Immediately?* I'll take it in the conference room!"

"At eight, Maddox. I'll be going now. Mr….waiter, is your foot?…"

"The heater, Mrs. Moloch, must have bumped it. It's okay. Thank you."

Hard to see her clearly. Sweat stung his eyes. Had she patted his arm? Better clean the slop off Moloch's desk. Oh Jesus, he had to pee. He'd wet his pants in Miss Brome's class, but that was kindergarten. Think of cement, wine corks, deserts…Dammit, waterfalls foamed everywhere.

That door, perhaps…Good, Moloch's bathroom. Hurry, voices. Moloch returning? What if he wanted to use?…Quickly, lock the door. That little button, shove…

*

"The bottom line, Schwingalt, is you don't know our real financial position. That's it, isn't it? Do we need to shift gears, adjust fuel? Are we on instruments or radar? Better check your panel. We don't want flameouts, a crash landing. Speak up man—*yes* or *no*?"

"I'd say on balance you're probably right, Maddox. However international operations promise a bonanza this year: oil, gas, textiles, food franchises. Pig-Out is becoming a global bonfire. Then with our High-Tech division, anything could—"

"*Howevers* and *anythings* won't wash, Schwingalt. *Bonanzas* are for quiz shows, jackpots. We're business, you're treasurer: guardian of the rainbowed pot. We want it full of gold, not bat guano. The buck stops with—"

"It stops with *us,* Maddox. We're in this together. Just remember that. Bankruptcy won't get *them* off our backs. The banks, the other creditors howling in the wilderness, are pussycats compared to that bunch."

"You're so right, Schwingalt. That was K. We're in trouble. It could get messy. Where is that blithering cart boy? Echewy vanishes, not a word. Think he'd leave instructions. No sense of responsibility. Ah, ten-fifteen. Must check…Miss Cuddy… Hmm, I'll be back in a bit, Schwingalt, just wait—"

"Very nice, Maddox, your Miss Cuddy. Is Miss Beamish on hold forever?"

"None of your business, Schwingalt. Have a sniff. The silver box on the table. May be the last for a long while. What's that racket? Must be Stoneball dropping dishes, shouting again. A house cleaning, top-to-bottom, is what we need. Burn the deadwood, flush out the incompetents."

Blithering cart boy. Carts: drummed up memories of other not so happy days. What had Pylor yelled at him once in high school algebra? Something about his numerators being wrong, denominators faulty. There was Pylor now, face emerging, filling the mirror on the door. "You'll fail, Stickle, if you don't get it. Is that what you want, *failure*?" Foam-flecks had gathered and sprayed from the corners of his mouth, dotted the exam results he was holding. "Life is just an equation, boy, one big algebra problem with a lot of variables. You'll be lost, gone forever if you get the wrong values, be a Shumley. He can't do it, Stickle, won't see the light: to him X equals *squat,* and Y *diddlysquat.* He'll end up pushing carts. Is that what you want, Stickle?: the broom and dustpan."

Had he shouted, knocked cologne on the floor? Was that a woman's voice coming from behind him? Some kind of handle

85

on the wall, a closet; perhaps another exit. He could leave unnoticed, return from the coffee room. Slowly, push...nothing. Maybe pull. Yes, opening. Careful, another room. Mirror flash of garter belt and high-heeled boot. His eyes, imagination? A man's voice—Moloch from across the room talking.

"Sorry, my love, bit of a problem. Can't explain now. Just time to sniff a spoon. The boots, lovely, add...hmmmm, so definite. And spurs that jingle jangle..."

"It's that man *K,* isn't it, Moley? He bothers you. I don't like it. Who is this Guzman he's told you to meet? Where's Katzenbach's. I—I've listened in before. Talk of gambling debts, drugs—a one time deal. Are you in trouble?"

"Piece of cake, Sweet. Ducks in a row. Nothing slips between old Moloch's buns. Why, there is absolutely nothing to worry—"

"Your wife, she seemed suspicious today. Last week too. Do you think?..."

"I'll have evidence on her corruption soon. Playing around, Shriker says. A regular buffet of sin from what I hear: consorting with moral lizards, the profligates in their fleshpots. No doubt believes it's her right. Talks as if I'm some sort of vacuum, black hole, a visionary cripple. Me, M and M, head of A.F. Yes, thank you, another toot might clear the horizon.

"Damn her Lib gibberish—extremist to the core, fascist. I can see it now, Cuddy: The march will begin with the bereaved widows from the southlands and move north. Broad-beamed battleaxes funded by billions in life insurance payoffs—they'll spread their plague across the country, world. Yes, annihilate, pulverize, anything that stands in their way: egos, philosophies, psychologies—the whole sheebang will be crushed beneath their platform heels. And Grunny?: she'll be carrying the flag, their leader—Big Foot herself, the Battleaxe incarnate."

"I understand, Maddox. You're almost a preacher, inspired. But my salary doesn't cover the other things we discussed. I'll need at least a thousand..."

"A thousand will fall at thy side, and ten thousand will go into your pocket. Have faith, Cuddy, I do. Big Foot will fall. I have a vision that soars beyond the world, the universe, a vision of love: love for them that side with us, the moral minority. God understands, will see to it that the rest, the hordes of human garbage that fester in ethical bankruptcy are hurled to the Devil, roasted on spits, consumed by dragons. That's what we all must do, every one of His creatures: get on with the job of getting *them*. That's God's will, and may I say mine, in a nutshell. Back at lunch. Yes, the boots...oh my yes..."

Why was the door tugging outward? On a pump spring? *No*, not a sneeze! Moloch was leaving. Hold it, just a few seconds...a moment..."Gahhsschoot...ahhshitt..."

"What the?...You!..."

"I'm sorry Mr. Mol..."

No use, Moloch would never listen. Shut the door, flush, out through the office.

"You there, what do you think?..."

"Good day, Mr. Schwingalt..."

The man was rabbitty: big ears, large teeth in the open mouth. Out to the elevators. Good, a light blinking, one stopping. Hurry, before Moloch...

"Nice jacket, Stickle. Or is it a dress? Looks absolutely— different."

"Priddle, what?..."

"Special assignment, old man. Eyes only and hush hush. Thought you were bagging groceries, stocking coolers. Must rush. Ciao."

Special assignment. Manila folder in his hand. Probly held yesterday's newspaper. No doubt roaming the halls to see if he could attract attention, project presence. Dammit, was Priddle talking to Moloch, pointing?...Elevator opening, the tall man beaming, clapping his shoulder.

"...So, Mr. Stickle, and how, might I ask, is the new job going?"

"Mr. Joblobber, I...the elevator...please hold...Go—I must...too late...I'm afraid Mr. Moloch just fired me."

"Fine, always—*fired?* Stickle's been holidayed, Ripstrom."

"Can't be helped. The system works. Unemployment is full time work. Cuts demand, inflation; stabilizes the structures. Honorable service."

"Mr. Moloch didn't exactly *fire* me, but under the circum- stances..."

How quickly Joblobber had dropped the *Mister.*

"There's no such thing as *not exactly,* Stickle, it's—"

"Mr. Futts, I can assure you…"

"To continue, Stickle, it's *either, or; yes, no; black or white; employed, unemployed.* Greys—the maybes, perhapses, *thinks,* all that qualifying rubbish—they waste time, cut profit, can't be programmed."

"Yes, Mr. Futts, you're right, but…"

"Here comes Mr. Moloch, Stickle. Suggest you zip your fly, get on parade."

"Ripstrom's right, Stickle. Chin up. It's a wonderful world out there. Smile, be glad you're alive, on vacation. What more could you ask? Have a happy. Bon voyage."

"I say there, Mr?…"

"Stickle, Mr. Moloch."

"Yes, Mr. Stickle. A bit excited back there, weren't we? Hmmm. Going down? Here we are, express."

"Yes…whatever, sir. The bathroom, I had to…hope you didn't?…"

"Not to worry. Down? Now, I don't know what that blasted—my wife—is paying you, but Miss Cuddy…It isn't what…None of your business, anyway. I think fifteen hundred for the photos would be sufficient. Agreed?"

"Mr. Moloch, believe me, I don't know your wife. I only met her a few minutes—"

"Two thousand. Let's say three, for *everything* you've got. Better still, *double* what she's giving you. Now…Where the hell are we? Pipes, that roaring…"

"Can't get in here without a pass!"

"What? I can't hear…"

"SECURITY, BASEMENT. CAN'T ENTER."

"I'M MOLOCH, PRESIDENT OF—"

"SHUMLEY'S THE NAME. RALPH'LL BE BACK. HE BE GONE. COMPLAINTS ON FOUR, SIX, TWELVE, FOURTEEN. SMELL COMIN' OUT THE GRILLS. PEOPLE ACTIN' STRANGE THEY SAY."

"SHUMLEY! NOT *STINKY* SHUM—"

"STICKLE! OLD H.S. REMEMBER?—"

BOTH IN THIS, ARE YOU? DON'T THINK…WHAT'S THAT "RINGING?"

"COULD BE 'MERGENCY. RALPH'D KNOW. JESS STEPPIN' IN FOR 'IM WHILES HE PEES. I'M ON CLEAN-UP. SAY,

88

'MEMBER OLD PYLOR, H. S. LAST REUNION, HEARD HE'S IN THE BUG HOME. JUMPED OFF A BRIDGE WITH THE GOLD WATCH OR SUMPIN. ALWAYS LIKED OLD PYLE. NEVER LIT INTO ME LIKE THEM OTHERS. GUESS HE SAWED I'D NEVER GO NOWHERE. IN THE BASEMENT SHOVIN' CARTS, PUSHIN' BROOMS. THAT'S ME. HAVE A NIP? 'BOUT THAT TIME."

"*SECURITY? DRINKING?* I'LL SEE TO IT YOUR WALKING PAPERS...WHAT IS THAT BANGING IN THE ELEVATOR?"

"DOAN KNOW. DOOR BE STUCK AGAIN. BUTTON F, THAT'LL DO'ER. THERE...IT'S THE MISSUS, H.S.— MUMS. I'D LIKE—"

"MIZ FART?—"

"AT THE DRINK AGAIN, ARE YOU STICKLE? WE WANT STAMPER. CRUMP SAYS 'RETURN FORM' NOT SIGNED."

"I...MIZ FARTLAR, THIS IS PRESIDENT MOLOCH...YOUR STAMPER—"

"BIG SHOT. I SEEN HIM ON COMPANY PICTURE. BRINGS IN WENCH. CUSTOMER DON'T LIKE WIREHEAD. CRUMP, ME AND HER NOT LEAVING. NO DEDUCTION NEITHER."

"*WENCH?* MY GOOD WOMAN, I HAVE NO IDEA...ARE YOU IN ON THIS? MISS CUDDY IS NO WEN...GET IT AWAY! JESUS CHRIST, *WHAT?*..."

"BART, DOWN FELLA. COME. BARTSEY'S OUR ATTACK MUTT. HALF WOLF, SHE BE. GO A HUNERD AN' EIGHTY POUND. WOULDN'T USE THE 'VATOR JUST YET, MR. MOLE. SHE NOT WORKIN'...DON'T SAY ISE DINT WARN...THERE GO THE POWER. 'Lectric's unglued. No needs to shout now. Gotta hit the backup engines. Your man, Muluck, be stuck probly 'tween floors. See Ralph comin' down the pike. Maybe he know..."

"Is he alright? Seems to be sliding against the wall."

"He be o'kay, H.S. Blind, though, almost. We's coverin' so's he can get full retirement next year. Gotta run. Switch transformers. To the right'n up. Spillway four'll doer. Gettcha out."

*

How long had he been lost? Hard to see. Just tiny lights in

crevices. Up two flights, down one ramp, then a second to this passageway. Was that the right count? He should be on about the same level as when he left Shumley. The corridor to his right might exit. The arrow on the rock, though, pointed up to the dripping pipes that snaked far into the gloom. Was that the sound of rushing water ahead? The door back there had read "EMERGENCY." For what? leading where? Better check...

Damn, the reddish bulbs behind were gone; greenish ones in front now dimming, flickering out. Wet, his feet soaked. Hands—a nipping, tugging...furry touchings at his head. Smell of sulphur, rotten eggs. Water rising to his waist, then afloat in current's pull. A foothold, on his feet again. That board, sign?: "DANGER BLASTING—POTHOLES." An explosion round the bend, shouts of laughter, falling rocks. Someone calling far ahead. Yes, it was Shumley, very faint. Everything was going to be alright. Good old Stinky.

"Shumley, I'm here. It's Stickle!"

Echoes fading into the distance. *Shumley Shumley Shumley ...here here here...*

"Who's it in the hole?"

"Me, Stinky, Stickle!" Good, he'd heard him.

"H.S.? We's lost Bart. Missus is huntin' level two."

"I'm lost, Shumley!"

"Found now. Bart's lost. Molux too. Went down, not up. We's lookin' for 'em both. Gotta check Cave Five."

"Shumley, I can't!..."

"Hear Bart howlin' on Chute Seven. Go there, H.S. She be up an' 'round, over the ramp and flyway. Gotta run. Battery on the ole bullhorn's dyin'."

"Shumley!..."

No use. If Stinky heard his voice, he wasn't lost, he was found. Shumley's algebra: a listener made all the difference—equalled *found* equalled *alive*. Even so, Stinky was gone for now, and he needed more information, signs...

A light glowing on the wall. Could it be?...Yes, button of some kind, perhaps the door to Chute Seven. Push it and...a peephole sliding open, intercom crackling. Inside, searchlights crisscrossing the darkness. Creatures—robots?—hundred of them stretching into the distance, frozen, staring blankly.

Was that a human caped in black on the scaffolding near the ceiling?: a conductor—arms whirling, gown swirling—directing operations? Motion at the glass: a forehead, nose, the bulging of an eye.

"Whackenberry here. We are off limits, a trespass zone. The hatchery is classified. You must have clearance—Red Pass."

Voice low, muffled. The face was backing off, a metal grin, the peephole closing. A growl behind him, claws that raked his back.

"Away! *Get away!*..."

"It just be Barty, H.S. He got the friendlies. No need to fear. Find prowlers sometimes nosin' 'bout the breedin' grounds."

"Shumley? Down boy, please..."

A flash of ivory, motor's purr.

"H.S., this here's Slue Nineteen. Cuts out Tunnel Four at Marly. Gotta run. Ralph says it's bad upstairs. Gas or sumpin'. Press the ole button—this un here. You be all set. Heel 'er up, Barto. We's off."

"But Shum...the robots?..."

Gone. Silence, not even footsteps moving off. Now a voice, a spidered shadow on the wall.

"I say, is someone there? This is Moloch, I'm *President* Moloch. Lost, I'm...Is that?...Whoever—*you*...Stickle, what?—"

"Whackenberry here. You are off limits, I repeat..."

"Whackenberry, it's me, Moloch! *Whackenberry!* What in God's name?...*Research:* your division is in the West. You had early retirement...rumors you died..."

"I'm calling security. You must evacuate immediately."

"Shumley at Box Four. Basement closin'. The kennels is openin'..."

"Over there, Stickle. That path must be the way! He's got more dogs!"

"No, Mr. Moloch, there's blasting down..."

Wouldn't listen. That disc glowing ahead must be the button Shumley'd mentioned. Good, an alley to the street. A figure perched on the trash bin ahead, fedora tipped low. Head rising slightly.

"Have a good one, Mr. Stickle? You look damp. Swimming?

Company pool?"

"Detective Karaki? No, I..."

"Won't be long now. Tying the knots."

"I've told you before, there's nothing to investigate, all an accident."

"We're more interested in the *other* thing, Mr. Stickle. *That's* no accident. Is Shumley in there?"

"Yes, but what does *he* have to do with anything?"

"Everything, Mr. Stickle, everything. Ciao."

Dizzy, better sit down, rest against the building. Close his eyes, breathe deeply. Somehow things would work out. After all, Moloch hadn't actually fired him. If he could just hang on until...

"Coffee break, Stickle?"

"No...Detective Fasten, I phoned..."

"Did you? Ramon was clever, Stickle. But he's gone. Found him in the garbage last night. *That* dumpster."

"What? *Murdered?* Who?..."

"Careful, if I were you. Could get messy. Shumley in there?"

"Yes, he—"

"Good. It's jelling. We'll get them. Suitcoat's wet, Stickle. Catch cold, die. Enjoy."

Enjoy? How to do that when the dots added up to only dots? Or perhaps weren't dots at all, or didn't exist. He was lost, alright. No one listening, not the right way, that was for sure. Connections?—he needed geometry, outline, then a higher math to figure value. Arithmetic, totals—they were inadequate. Pylor had short-changed him somewhere, left him with a cartful of goodies and nowhere to shove them except...

There was Manny's across the street. Should he go in and inquire about his date? Nice to carry on a simple conversation with someone. Might help to clear his head. Talking sometimes did that. Other times, like recently, what he said seemed to meet invisible walls, rebound and jam his head till it became an angry hive. Yes, he'd see what Manny had arranged. Maybe it would be just what he need...

"BREWBUSTER, THE BEER THAT NEVER QUITS. FA LA *LA* LA LA LA, LA LA LA LA."

Why didn't *he* quit, though, take early retirement, get out. Was it money? After all, Ethel might decide to abandon him for Rolf. But benefits, the annuity—there would be enough. The tin cup and broom weren't really a threat. Might it be unemployment?: the word, sour, a whispered curse. Yet hadn't Futts called it honorable service? It seemed more like a sin, though, unjustified existence. Perhaps it was fear: scared he'd become nothing, lose his *Stickleness* without Company. *Nothing* was being dead in a way, wasn't it? Bad algebra, indeed. No, he wasn't ready for that yet, not quite.

10

"WOULD *SIR* CONSIDER a Manny's hairpiece? The Executo mustache, perhaps? Lends authority, that decisional look we all crave."

"No, I don't believe it would help—work, I mean."

"Work schmurk. On she goes. Don't be fraidy. Smile for mirror now."

"I *told* you..."

Could a hairpiece do that? Twenty years younger at least.

"Sir likes? Now for mustache. The Stroker is *smashing*... Here, let me...See?—macho macho."

"Please, I could never wear..."

Who was that stranger eying him? Hair, a wing of jet at the forehead, lip bristling defiance. It wasn't Stickle, old H.S.

"May I say, sir, stunning. Here's Matchmaker's dateroo. It's all on the print-out. Yes yes. Could we interest you in a little pep potion—lovelift—if you know what I mean? Over here, behind the curtain. Breathe deeply when I break the capsule. Marvelous, is it not? Puts a tiger in your tank, oh it does!"

"Bitter smell. What is it?"

"Our best selling line: Zoom. Thirty of the little darlings, would that be enough?"

"Really, it isn't necessary. If you'll give me the bill, that will...On second thought, I'll take them. That woman—the cardboard model, your advertisement: *Walking, Talking, Life-Size Playmate*—what?...So...so naked. I mean attractive—the bikini..."

"Sir, likes? Mustn't touch. That's Suzy Q. We have a line in Fred and Ralph too."

"No, I don't want..."

Had he run his hand over the poster in the area of the model's seat? She seemed alive, ready to speak, move...

"Would you like black, brown, yellow or white? We have Jocko too. Forgot *him*. Gorgeous legs, biceps like grapefruit."

"Jocko? Why would I want?...Yes, a Suzy, a white..."

Face felt flushed. It was warm in Manny's. A *Suzy:* Had he really?...

"Would sir prefer to wear his novelties?"

"No, I...might as well."

Getting hotter. A funny sensation in his thighs and rising. The woman in the ad smiled, winked at him. He'd go home, contact his date. Perhaps they'd do more than talk. Something a little more romantic might be in order: city lights, dancing, perhaps drinks. And then who could tell?—a spark, fireworks? Anything was possible. Even in his life.

*

Strange how the savaged apartment seemed to possess a certain beauty, a mosaic of destiny, his fate if he wasn't careful.

"Do a bit of damage don't you, Stickle, when you tie one on?"

"Pardon? Mrs. Gribbley, I...it *is* a bit of a mess." Had he been standing in the open doorway? "It isn't what you think, Mrs. Gribbley, you see—"

"*See* alright. When the cat's away, the mouse will play. Puts on some extra whiskers and a fur cap and does God only knows."

"Mrs. Gribbley, damn it all, I'm not a mouse."

"Foul mouth too. Don't forget *Hickory Dickory Dock*, Stickle. That one fell. Your likes always do. The clock may strike for you. And then the Devil will be waiting. My Fred in all his born days never took a drink, never went near a woman, why he…"

"He married *you,* Mrs. Gribbley."

"I'm not a woman. Not *that* kind."

"I'm sure, Mrs. Gribbley. Fred was a lucky man."

"You bet he was, and I never let him forget it till the day he died. Why, on his deathbed, his almost last words were about me. 'Mums,' he said, 'I'm so lucky!' Then he died."

"He surely was, Mrs. Gribbley, to die—I mean about you. I must go. Goodbye."

Entering the apartment was somewhat like wandering into his own mind in recent days: a random mix of this and that with crazy patterns everywhere—a mod design, the different look. Mattress, sofa—his special chair—all slashed in violent swirls with tongues of stuffing bursting through as whitish flames that warmed the scene. It was indeed a mix of old and new, an experimental art that…

What was the matter with him! *Art, beauty!*—it was a godawful pigsty. When would *Miz Trench*—Ethel—be back? Was that really him in the mirror? Mr. Hair—The Mustache—a contender, not wimp or mouse.

There, the magazine on the floor, that man on the cover, *him,* Horace Stickle, karate stance: crouched, arms extended —lithe, lethal. And the man had a mustache, hair too, lots of it, shocked upwards as his arms struck out. Easy, he could do it: tense, bend, strike. *Hah!* Had he yelled, fallen? Was that why he was on the floor? Must have gotten carried away, lost his footing.

Objects floated to-and-fro with colors weaving, dancing in a nervous light that trembled round the dusky room. His lady, evening's promised date, all gowned and regal beckoned at the window laced in snow, then waved and laughed and turned away.

Had he become unhinged? Woman at the window and all that claptrap! Only a reflection of himself, the new mophead to be unleashed upon…Where was the Matchmaker printout? Had it in his hand when…On the floor by the magazine, in two pieces. His judo chop must've… *Yes folks, with a single blow the man will separate this sheet of paper into…* Seemed to be a form letter. Hard to focus his eyes. Hold it up to the light.

Dim. Had to get brighter bulbs.

Dear Customer:
Matchmaker has picked your lucky lady. It is our policy not to reveal personal info such as phone, address, and name for obvious reasons. Believe us she is the winner. It—she will be at Julio's Bar and Dance at 7 pm for the next 2 nites. She will be in a red dress in one of the booths near the dance floor. When you speak to her mention us, Manny's, and if all goes well as expected you can exchange all the intimate info you want. We have done all to assure a perfect match. Lotsa luck and refer your friends. If you're not satisfied come back. Remember trying again is succeeding.

Manny

P.S. When you try again there is another fee.

Somehow there was a familiar ring to the letter. If you return, *deduction*. Was the spelling bad? Maybe his eyes, tired. A "Zoom" might help. What had the clerk done to the tablet, cracked it? Yes, now sniff. He'd straighten up the apartment later. His job, Company? Slipped his mind. Tomorrow would be soon enough. Moloch, would understand. First day on the job: there were always problems. Perhaps his luck was changing. "Your barometer is rising, Mr. Stickle, skies are clearing, better weather ahead, sir."

The stranger in the mirror saluted; disappeared momentarily, then reappeared as someone he might have known, perhaps a faded copy of himself. The figure turned slowly and walked away. Effect of the tablet, a mirage in the wasteland of his mind? Not important. The man with the hair and mustache was going in the opposite direction, out the door and into the night. For he had an appointment to keep. And who could tell?: It might change his whole life. It just very well might.

✳

The two drinks on the way to Julio's had made him buoyant and warm. His first date came to mind. Who had she been? Little Erlene Ninninger, that was it, her. A tiny child with no center to her eyes, it had seemed. He'd spotted them finally,

98

though: pinpoints of grey behind the glasses, lenses steamy, thick. It hadn't been so good, had it? Still could remember her only question: "Why do they call you *horseshit?*" Should see him now: man of the night on his way to rendezvous, a neon cowboy riding tall as he entered the Bar and Dance of Julio's.

That must be his scarlet woman in the end booth, back to him, red hat, dress to match. A man talking to her. The lady's head shaking. Good, she was the one, waiting for him. He'd tap her shoulder, then...

"Manny's, Miss Manny, I mean..."

"My goodness, we're a bit late, aren't we. Must always try to be punctual, yes we must. For heaven's sake, don't hide behind me, sit down. Not over there, *here,* longside."

"Yes, of course, I wasn't thinking..."

Thinking wasn't the problem, focusing his vision was. Garish rainbows speared the smoke, converged, exploded, sprayed the room in tempo to the music's blast. She was big, maybe tall, his head barely clearing her shoulder. He'd asked for *petite, blond.* Hard to see anything under her bonnet: a scarlet tent that shadowed face and tinged it blue.

"Let me introduce myself, I'm..."

"Not to say, my good man. Before that we should get to know each other a bit, talk, have a dance. Hmmmm, you seem small. Asked for something larger. But then small men interest me. There's a psychology about them that needs studying. Are you there?"

"What? I'm here. Yes, surely. Big women certainly have to be considered too...ah, in the light of their bigness. Why my—"

Wife. The word almost erupted. Better watch...

"You're married? I thought so. Don't be embarrassed. We all make mistakes. Henry was mine: had no spine. Stayed in the same job for years, never took a stand, soldiered, gave me what I wanted."

"I see, but—"

"You don't appear to be a *Henry.* Henry was bald, fat, never conditioned. Drank beer and watched cartoons on Saturday. A bowl of porridge, putterer. Frittered himself right out of our relationship. His bad luck though, not mine. Luther, my psychiatrist—you should try him—cracked the nut. A man of steel. And you, my munchkin, are you a man?

Speak up. Up up up. Don't be shy. I'll listen, hear you out."

The woman made him nervous: a prosecutor, jury, judge. What would the sentence be? Had he committed a crime? The hat might hide a hangman's noose, worse. What had she asked? Head turning towards him, hat bearing down.

"Well, I think—"

"You think! Don't believe? You don't *believe* you're a man? Maybe a woman then? What you think isn't necessarily what you believe, or vice versa. Neither may represent fact. How do you like that? What *are* the facts, you little dumpling? Or don't you know? Maybe you're confused. That man approaching, do you?—"

"Excuse me, may I have this dance?"

"No, certainly not, I'm with somebody."

"That's what I mean, your *somebody,* the gentleman. My name is Ralph. I..."

"Please, no. *No,* I'm with the lady."

"Terribly sorry, I just thought you...it seemed...another time perhaps..."

The woman seemed uneasy, drink gone in a swallow. The hands on her glass, large, catchers' mitts. Quickly back in her lap. No doubt mistaken: doves rustling together, silken and white in their crimson nest. The hat again dipping towards him, a breeze, the odor of garlic—mint?

"That man, *Ralph*—do you know, associate with his type? Is *he* what you call a man?"

"No, I've never seen...go out...He's different, that's all. We're all men. You, me...I mean man, *man.* Miss?..."

"Not to get pushy with names. Talk first, then dance. Maybe names later. Ah yes, finally a slow one."

"I'm not very good. Would rather just sit..."

She hadn't heard. Already sliding out, her thigh sweeping him sideways to his feet. At least five inches taller, even in flats. Striding ahead, she consumed the room in a reddish haze. Then onto the dance floor, stumbling, a band of iron at his arm, tugging him upright, lifting...The music stopping, a voice blaring.

"A little early folks, but this is our Julio Special. For two weeks prior to New Years Eve the lucky couple in the spotlight kiss under the mistletoe and get a free supper. And where will it land? Where oh where?...The lady in red and the gentlemen..."

Light exploding. Whiteness stabbing at his eyes, a drumbeat roll. Roaring crowd pressing hard on every side. Was she bending?...Hat, a flaming saucer whirling down? And then her arms were jammed around him, his face being lifted upwards upwards towards a bluish moon that swooped down low. And for an instant lip met lip while arms encircled, tightened, then released. Had he closed his eyes? There on the floor, his Executo perched on the crown of her hat. The spotlight moving away.

"Mr. Stickle!"

" *Mawlsey...Miss*—Hen...I mean...It's time...go, I must see to it...other things...Excuse me..."

"It's alright, Mr. Stickle, you silly goose! No need to turn tail..."

A man touching his arm, tugging...

"Ralph again. I thought maybe?..."

The street, the night, closed in with fishnet maze of blink and flash that caught him up and held him fast.

Henry, Henrietta. He'd kissed a man, and dammit, he'd...he'd sort of...didn't mind? But it—*she*—was a woman. Or had the—whatever—changes been finalized? Even so, did you really become a man or a woman or anything else by changing your body? No matter, he, Horace Stickle, was a man. He might be *horseshit, loser, mouse;* but he was still a man. Who could deny that? Who?...

He was off balance, felt the sidewalk tilt. Or was it his Executo. Yes, it had slipped over one ear. The Dungeons Bar on his left. A drink to settle his nerves, lasso his brain. Maybe two...

"Scotch and soda please."

Weird clothing: leather glistening, stud and chain. A voice, paw extended, hairy face.

"New here, sweetheart? What a yummy rug you have! Little off center, luv. Let Fredricka—you can call me Freddy—fix."

Voice shrill, giggly.

"No thank you...leaving...must really go..."

The scream of singers, crash of band from down the bar. Spotlights knifing through the haze; a stage where riders

101

gunned their bikes and fisted smoke. Quick, down his drink and hurry out.

Hand on coat, the voice a rasp: "Dime, Mister, could you spare something? A quarter?..."

"Mawsley will surely dump me now."

"Too bad, mister. Thanks, thanks a lot."

"I kissed him. Kissed a *Henry* ..."

"Hope it works out, Mister. Ciao."

A preview of what he faced in years to come?: to roam the streets as Futts had warned with tin cups, pencils, wheezing breath. An outcast, no-collar bum: rags in transit, pauper's grave.

That's the way we found him, officer. Pennies over both eyes, a quarter in one hand; this here pelt or sumpin in the other. He froze solid, like concrete.

Anybody know this man?

I do officer. Gribbley, the name's Maud Gribbley. That's Stickle. Down he fell and freezed his crown; hickory dickory, hickory dock. Why my Fred—

Thank you mam. Get your statement later. Bag 'im Louie.

How had he arrived in mid street? Cars a spray of bullets whizzing by. Screech of brakes, face at window glistening red, fist balled and shaking, mouth agape.

Where was the beggar? Run and weave. A bus, great engine bearing down; the driver helpless, hanging on, head a blackened pea on high that shook and nodded violently.

Moloch. There was President Moloch up the street amongst a crowd in evening dress where uniform and braid bobbed to-and-fro, where fields of glass, a midnight ice, rose and towered to the night. Was Moloch staring his way? What did it matter?: He had his whiskers and rug. Snug as a bug in a rug. Control, he must keep...Moloch was likely his last chance for reprieve—President Moloch, that scaffolding of black disappearing into Harbor View, the name ablaze in rainbow script.

Mawsley would probably dispose of him in time—maybe even tomorrow—on one pretext or another. His face would forever be an embarrassment in the office, a blot she would want to erase. Moloch might prevent that termination and place him elsewhere. He'd seemed a bit friendly at the elevator earlier, hadn't he? Wanting to talk about photos or something.

Difficult to recall. Perhaps he could speak to him alone for a minute, explain the Mawsley thing and the retraining problem. People were reasonable. Moloch as chairman would be logical, hopefully compassionate. Men with great power usually had a greater wisdom, depth, than the ordinary man. It only seemed natural.

"He'll listen, understand, I'll explain it all." Doorman nodding. "I am not a mouse!"

"No *sir.*"

"Thank you. That will be all. I'm going in."

*

"You have a table, sir? The Revolution Room requires reservations." The waiter squat and very close.

"No, I'm looking..."

Fields of glitter sparkled past; figures glided checkered routes: a game of pass, receive and tricky plays that scored on silver tray and gleaming plate.

"Perhaps to join a party?"

"Yes, that's it, right. Moloch, a Mr. Moloch."

"Of course, Mr. *Maddox* Moloch and wife. The Tilversmiths."

He had the ball. Now, let his blocker lead the run. Off and coasting left and right, then up the middle, first down, ten; closer closer to a score. What to say or do once there? More to point, the question: why? To win, survive, to make a play? A hand on shoulder—penalty?

"To wait here, sir, we're rounding Tower Turn, East View Harbor. Magnificent, is it not?"

Turning softly in the night, a saucer rimmed in candlelight. Was that from a poem? Next he'd be into Martians, lasers, extraterrestrial lore. Better watch his roving head, the loops and twists were breaking free.

"Sorry to forget, sir—your name?"

"Horace, it's..."

"An extra chair. Moment please. There. Mr. Horace to join your party, Mr. Moloch."

"Who? You must be mistaken, I don't know this man."

"Actually you do, Mr. Moloch. Very sorry to barge...At the elevator...wanted to talk to me today...Lost, we got lost

103

in the basement...Bart, he tried to attack you. The photos, Mr. Moloch...I never...Then Guzman...I overheard...by mistake, in the bathroom. All a mistake. But I want you to know...I didn't mean to kiss Henry, I mean Mawsley, Miss..."

"*Kissed*... Who in the name?... *You. Guzman...* You're with— part of *that* too?"

"Name's Tilversmith. Any friend of Maddy's is good enough for me. Fertilizer's my game. Yours?"

"Football. No, it's Amalgamated, I'm there."

Tilversmith, a barracuda perched on its tailfin. Rows of teeth, deadly grin. The wife, practically invisible to his left: a wisp of hair, rising fork.

"Photographs? Maddox, what is all this?"

"Nothing, dear. Hunting trip. Elk. Some pictures."

"My good man, may I ask?...You have a resemblance..."

"Yes, Grunulda, I'm *sure* you've both...Maybe not. Work incognito, do you, Mr. Stickle?"

"Mr. Moloch, if we could just have a moment alone...Realize this is an improper time..."

"Bagged a moose myself up North last year, Maddox. Bigger'n a bus. Antlers over the fireplace. Makes the whole house a home. Why—"

"The photographs, Mr. Stickle. I am *extremely* interested. Guzman—that's Katzenbach's. We'll make arrangements at the Parlor on *everything.* About noon tomorrow. What the!..."

"Another tremor, dear? Or just shaky? Your drink spilled. Now about these photographs, Mr?..."

"Stickle, Mrs. Moloch. I'm not sure myself just what Mr. Moloch means..."

"Little old jiggle there, Maddox. Down south we had a gasser. She swallowed a town. Sssshwhop, all gone. Let me tell—"

"I'm sure, Tilversmith. Now...We seem to be moving faster. Waiter, is there?..."

"Can't say, sir. The tremors...Could be the main spindle. The Rumsden men were in about *top-spin* today. Slanner would know. Excuse..."

"I must go, Mr. Moloch. Apologies for the interruption. Katzenbach's at noon, then. I surely hope everything works..."

The restaurant was definitely moving faster. Hardly noticed

it before. A frisbee whirling its way atop the city. Things were coming together. Moloch cared, saw him as a human being, not just as Cart Boy. He was losing his balance, another man tottering too, stumbling toward him, grabbing at his hairpiece, pulling...

"How nice, Stickle. Shall we dance. Heh. Gather this fungus belongs to you."

"Priddle, you bloody!...Evening, Mr. Futts, Joblobber. Just leaving..."

"Mr. Moloch, a pleasure. Bob Joblobber is the name. My associate, Ripstrom Futts. We're Snatly, Broadspringer, the Blue Book Reorganization. We seem to be...Ah, good, slowing down."

"Gentlemen? The Blue Book?...You *know* Mr. Stickle?"

"Mr. Moloch, *President* Moloch, I'm Priddle, *Festin* Priddle. Might I say, Stickle here has been with Amalgamated for twenty-five years. He's not done much in the way of advancing—"

"Let me fly that kite a bit higher, Festin."

"Fine, Bob, I was just—"

"You mean to say, Mr. Stickle—*Stickle*—is an employee? He isn't?..."

"Quite true, Mr. Moloch. The Cart Boy position was to preserve his benefits until he qualifies for *Peanut* or *Mouse.* Glad to see you are getting along so well."

"An *employee.* Thank you. Evening, gentlemen. Mr. Stickle, I *know* you have other business. Let me see you to the elevators. Waiter, boy, another round of the same."

"I'm Grunulda Moloch, Mr. Stickle. Shame about the service spill this morning. Not to worry, though. You'll see."

"Thank you, Mrs. Moloch, kind of you to say so."

" *This* way, Stickle."

"Mr. Moloch, I certainly appreciate—"

"I don't, Stickle—evening, Rathbone—appreciate anything you've done. Your last paycheck will be in the mail tomorrow. Deception does not pay, Stickle. One of life's lessons. Good night."

"Mr. Moloch, I thought..."

Moloch leaving, pivoting, striding away: a band of black shooting into the chandeliers, growing smaller, narrower, now a dot. Clouds of specks pinwheeling the room, rushing toward him, sucked into his head...

"Sir is going down?"

"Sorry, what?..."

"Down, sir would like?..."

"Thank you, yes...down, I'm going down, leaving, going out. But I am not a mouse!"

"To say *not,* sir. Surely not."

*

Someone talking. A spotlight glaring in the dark. "Hello there, I'm Strange Shirly. Do you think I'm pretty? I think you're just boffo."

The apartment, home? How, when? A minute ago, ten hours? *Strange Shirly.* Had he put that video on? Where was the football tape? Something across his lap. Stretched almost to the other end of the couch. Rubber...a doll, big one...The Suzy-Q. Pull it off him...

"Do you like my legs? Strange Shirly has beautiful legs, no?"

"Hello, I'm Suzy. Bet you don't know what *Q* stands for. Find my secret button and you'll have a surprise."

The thing talked. Must've touched a switch.

"Horace! Is that you? Can't see a thing. The lights—there. What in?...That!...on your head, lip?..."

"Ethel, I didn't expect..."

"You know why they call me Strange Shirly? It's because I'm really *Sam,* not Shirly. Let me show..."

"Two days, Horace and that that...doll, perversion...Have you gone?—"

"Hello, I'm Suzy. Bet you don't know..."

"Give me that. You look drunk. Where did you ever get?..."

"...There, you did it. See, I'm not a Suzy at all. My real name is Sonny. Look between my..."

"Pure filth, Horace. Moral sleaze. Have you nothing to say?"

"Yes dear, Mr. Moloch fired me and I kissed Henry. But I am not a mouse."

"I'm not going to reply, Horace. I'm going to a hotel. Apparently you need time to straighten *everything* out. I would hope mother's urn is *not* in this mess."

106

"I could explain all this, Ethel, but I'm tired, exhausted."

"I'll bet you are. A circus, Mrs. Gribbley says. Criminals, crazies from a bar—gutter riffraff. She caught me at the door. We talked. I know: a last hurrah, the fling. No wonder you were fired. Others fare worse, Horace. You can count yourself fortunate. Gribbley says Snoley's gone with gout. Something to investigate, a job possibility—building janitor. Employment abounds: delivering, chauffeuring, shoveling— the works. A merry-go-round of opportunity spins, Horace. Grab the ring, be glad it's there and consider yourself lucky."

"Lucky! I've lost everything—"

"And gained the world. It's a new age, Horace. Roles are changing, the work place too. In time we may reside in an electronic cottage. I've had my eye on a tract in Weederville. Read the new futurists. We might become 'prosumers.' You could grow our dietary needs. My job could be handled on a console. Flex time would take care of the rest. You could paint, write—maybe fiction, poetry; study piano, violin, guitar; try sculpturing, meditation. Everything you ever wanted would be at your fingertips. By having no status you would be among the new elite—the eccentrics. You'd be a no-name celebrity. Forget your silly ideas of finding all this—the good life—at Amalgamated."

"Silly! I've spent my life—"

"To finish. Then you can go back to Sonny and Sam. Being home persons, we could adopt. A secret, Horace: We support a dark child in the East through Foster Parents—Amin Mugabe, a lovely boy. We could bring him here. You could have the son you always wanted, play in the garden. He could help you plant the zucchini, tomatoes, potatoes! I hear some people are even raising livestock. The future's unlimited, Horace. As one writer says: The waves are upon us. Get your surfboard, my dear, and as the young ones advise: *hang ten.* It's a wonderful time—"

"*Muga what?* Grow potatoes?! *Poetry?* Have you gone mad?..."

It was as though she had suddenly suggested that all the familiar luggage and furniture of his life be junked, that he don overalls, grab a pitchfork and toss manure with a black creature from another world. *An eccentric no-name celebrity.*

What did that mean? To join a nudist colony? Keep odd pets like fleas, an anteater? Wear funny hats and develop a twitch?

Grand larceny of his life was in the air, another equation he couldn't balance, retraining of a different kind for which he wasn't fitted. What she was suggesting made his past seem unconnected, wasted. And future bliss (would it be that?), a victory gained without fight or sacrifice—a mousey honor indeed: heaven with a breath mint, or utopia in the sparkle of a toilet.

"Strange Shirly has a friend, Ralph, who'll visit me in a few minutes. But first..."

"Ethel, what about the woodsplitter, rockbuster? How is *your* Ralph?"

"Rolf, it's *Rolf,* and that's none of your business. He is under therapy. It...ask Strange Shirly, Horace. Perhaps all of you could use the same doctor. Don't know how lucky the lot of you are. Want to become women? Takes a real man to be a woman, Horace. Don't you ever forget it. I must be off. Take...be careful, Horace. Goodnight."

She hadn't looked too good. Tired? The job not all it was cracked up to be? Did he feel anything for her anymore? She seemed so remote, like a foreign land he might have glimpsed in some travel magazine: bleak terrains of craggy peaks that huge birds cruised. But then what about himself? How describe his new found country of Shirly, Suzy, dance and bar?: sad, perhaps, like garbage dumps where things that might have been, or were, lay strewn helter skelter, piled on high: the fallout from Futts's New Age, or just himself, his junkyard brain. Outside the door, the click of heels, and Gribbley's walker thumping down the hall. Now a voice, a squawk arising from the clutter on the floor:

"That's my *by-by button,* sweet. Till next time, love from Sonny and Suzy. Ciao."

The face became a corrugated mask that grinned and shrivelled in the fading glow from the T.V. Moonlight striped the room and touched the mirror opposite him with silver strands.

Mirror, mirror, on the wall,
Was Fred the luckiest of them all?

What about himself? Hadn't the wheel of fortune just ticked

off his number? Wasn't Ethel suggesting that the millenium was almost upon him? That he would likely soon be free to dabble and putter about at whatever he wanted for the rest of his life? Why then wasn't he ecstatic, doing cartwheels? Why was it he felt—what?: confused, scared? Appalled was more like it.

But wasn't this one dream of democracy, the System?: to have computers and robots churn out the good life for everyone?—do away with work. Then they could all get down to the really important job of perfecting themselves, or each other, into a just and noble brotherhood of happy souls. Trouble was, how did you determine success, being ahead, having what it took, in that enterprise? Who were the New Enterpreneurs, Flat-outers, Cranners, in that world? How did you produce or package the product? Or was that just a crazy obsession for status? Besides, the whole idea seemed boring, a perfect time for catastrophe, visitors from space—a surprise party.

Possibly religion, that stranger to his life, had the answer. But then there was a spiritual carnival out there, therapies for every ill. Massage parlors galore. Things *happened* to people, no guilt was fixed: the cause, a mutant gene or not breast fed. Evil, sin? —just words, a Trivial Pursuit, perhaps a Scrabble fit. Nothing real, not chimneys, smoke; a black that crept within, without, and absolute: the Light, should it exist, reversed to pitch— empty sockets, grinning skull.

Were new designs of *Peanut, Mouse,* the next apocalypse in time, a Second Coming, living Chip, organic, mapping programs like the mind? And if not that, what then?: the infinity of acts in endless plays of which Joblobber spoke glowingly?

Would that not depend on the fate of the present production, the kind of *splink* that drew the curtain down? Indeed, he well could be an icicle that shot the stars, a silver bullet streaking night in frozen search. And should he strike a target in the candlelight, what then?: find Priddle there to wave him on, a sheet of black marks in his hand?

Shadow stretched across the room, a graveyard mounding in the night. Cemeteries, death—the broken urn. He'd return to Katzenbach's for a replacement tomorrow.

109

Maybe he'd bump into Moloch. Hadn't the man talked of a meeting with Guzman? Maybe A.F. was going to add the funeral business to its other interests. Yes,that was it: He'd straighten things out with the funeral director, Moloch too. The President had blamed him for deception. He'd explain about the hairpiece and mustache. Mawsley as well. As for the new urn, he'd stock it with dust if they couldn't find Mums. Ethel would never know the difference.

Maybe that was the secret of happiness: to never know the difference. But dammit, he did—at least he thought he did—most of the time. And perhaps, if anything,that was his luck, or lack of it.

11

"GOOD MORNING. My name is Stickle, Horace Stickle. I'd like to speak to a Mr. Guzman. It's about an urn that's lost— broken, I mean. Sat on it. I'd like to purchase a new one, blue..."

The woman, who had appeared in housecoat and mules, nodded toward a corridor where candles glowed dully in the shadows.

"Sshh, bereaved are down there—the Croners."

"Sorry."

"It's alright. Don't really believe in death anyway. You'll see. They'll invent a pill."

"I suppose..."

Hard to tell if she was the same woman as before. Face hidden, a lump of white in frizzled nests. Earphones on, radio clipped to her pocket. Whiff of gin.

"Yes, life goes on again here, there, wherever. Know what I mean? Love this song: Earl Wrangler—*Big Boy Up Yonder.* Coffee?"

"No, thank you. Ashes, there was a problem..."

"Guzy's in the Cold Room right now. Up in a jot. I'm

temporary. Gretchen's got the bug. Going around. Bear it'd bite you. Hee. Pardon. Place's creepy, gives me the giggles. I'll take you to the Sample Room. Browse if you like. A drink?: Snoram's rules."

"No—well, a whiskey?..."

"Coming up. Rocks, straight up, mix?"

"Rocks, that would be fine. Noon, almost lunchtime. Never drink before—"

"Here we are. Right through the door at the end. Like I said, Snory's in the freezer. He'll be up at red light. Enjoy."

Difficult to see objects in the gloom. Needed more than tiny lights buried in the ceiling. They cast an orangish glow, distorted colors, made his face burn darkly in the mirror looming over the mantelpiece. There, behind glass, urns: lion, eagle, squirrel, rabbit, beer stein, sportscar, celebrities...Wouldn't do at all. Plain ones, where?...On the other side, around the partition? No, coffins: open, sleek, gleaming and waiting—reptiles shadowed, prey certain...Voices across the hall.

"Anyone else here, Mr. Guzman?"

"Nobody important: a loose end to tie. We do that, Mr. Moloch. Very efficiently. The knot is *permanent.* Took our property, wouldn't make amends. Sound familiar?"

"Where?..."

"In the lounge, other end. Just came in a few minutes ago. But not your concern."

A loose...him? Not a mouse this time, a *loose end,* something definitely worse. Should have followed up the call to Fasten. *Trafficking, fifteen years.* Crazy not to have realized...urn, drugs...Fasten, come to think of it, had implied Guzman and Zalt were accomplices: connections he hadn't made, Foch's neurons in flight. Must get away immediately. They'd spot him, though, from across the hall. Another exit, perhaps...

"We'll go to the Sample Room, Mr. Moloch. More privacy. This is Operations Control. Flow charts, graphics, data—all at one's fingertips. Everything calibrated to the finest technology. Completely computerized. Hookups planned nationwide. Efficient, wouldn't you say?"

No time. Coffin his only chance. Don't slam the lid. Open a crack. Good. Had his drink too. Satin, a tiny pillow, ruffles: quite nice. *Nice.* If they caught him, it was *knot. Deduction* was

112

bad enough; but could he survive *knot?* Doubtful.

"K is unhappy, Mr. Moloch. That is unfortunate, very. We must do better. *Much.* You would agree?"

The voice guttural, close. There, almost beside him, eyes that glittered, raisin pips. Head barely level with the coffin—a gnome in black.

"I've made every effort—"

"Effort doesn't count, Mr. Moloch. Without results who can predict what may happen? Things that go bump in the night might collide with *you.* There could be an explosion, injury. Worse."

"Are you threatening?..."

"Explaining, Mr. Moloch, counselling. Mr. K has instructed that you will be employing an executive assistant—Strom. His credentials are impeccable. In time capital will be issued to new buyers, personnel replaced, budgets revised. S will oversee high technology operations, in particular; require data on current research, investment—hmm, that sort of thing. Information, the proper kind—military, other—is the new drug, Mr. Moloch. The right people, governments, pay handsomely."

"You're crazy, Guzman, that's treason. You can be shot, get life. Why I wouldn't—"

"Oh, but you *will,* Mr. Moloch. You *want* life. That's why you'll cooperate. *Shot* is for amateurs."

Did he dare take a drink? *Shot, knot.* Rhymed. Moloch loomed by the urns mopping his face, head near the ceiling. Never fit in a regular coffin. Guzman limped toward the casket. One shoe outsized, heel thick. Hand reaching out, moving back-and-forth on the lid.

"Treason, Mr. Moloch? Who's to know? Intelligence activities of government are a porridge of overlapping nonsense programmed for maximum inefficiency. We'll be on the inside looking out, while they're intercepting tapes of cocktail chatter in foreign limousines. No, Mr. Moloch, we needn't worry about *them.* Our, shall we say, little home on the range is quite safe. Now—*Gentlemen?* This is a private conference. We will be through shortly."

"Only a minute, Mr. Guzman. We need a Mahogany Corona for the Newly Entombment: a Golgotha Pageant, this afternoon."

"Of course. He's in Prince Vault on hold. Be quick. Transact the accounting in control."

"Yes, right away, Mr. Guzman."

He was being lifted, lid clicking shut. Luck was with him this time. Once they put him down, he'd get out fast. Blasted drink sloshing all over. A bump, voices moving away...Damn top was stuck. Push harder. Pound the sides, yell. Nothing. Silence. Be calm; they'd have to open up for Newly. No problem. Breathe slowly, conserve air. Everything would be alright. Others talking,coming closer. Shout, bang again.

"That Granger?"

"Yes, a Red Dot Leader on Printout Two—the Mahogany. We're running late."

"Thought we'd already ashed Croner."

"Later, this afternoon. Hurry it up."

Was he on rollers, moving? *Granger*... An explosive whoosh. A roaring underneath that warmed the coffin, made him sweat.

Cigars and chimneys, furnace fed; Stickle in a basket, charred and dead. Punched out today, but not hooray.

Another epitaph that left something to be desired. His shouts drowned in a rushing whoosh that...

Jolting, falling, then a crash that sprung the lid. Out and to the stairwell on his right. Floor a sinking, rising, gelatin. Tremors, it must be...Down one flight and several more. Walls and steps, crumbling stone; mossed and greasy, sulphur stench. Blackness lit by pinpoint bulbs that flickered greenly overhead: cat eyes watching, tracking every move.

Suddenly a dazzling white unfurled: a room that stretched on endlessly. Empty? No, a speck, a table, rising, floating near with figure perched at corner's edge. Perhaps his eyes, the sudden light...

"Mr. Stickle, glad you dropped in." The voice a distant, muffled bleat.

"Detective Karaki? Is it?..."

The silhouette, a sliver, black, that pierced the white. A gleam of metal, something draped.

"Of course, Mr. Stickle. Poison, you know."

"Poison?"

"Yes,the autopsy proved it conclusively: chocolates. She ate the whole box—Mrs. Granger. We have suspects, Mr.

Stickle. Oh yes: Mr. Joblobber's affair with her. Futts's jealousy over the relationship. Joblobber and Futts are, hmm, that way. Perhaps *you* have similar, ah?..."

"Are you *suggesting*?—"

"Not to become excited, Mr. Stickle. We know, have the facts. Manny's, it was raided—Detective Fasten's squad. Your name was found. Do you recall a Mawsley, a.k.a., Henrietta, otherwise Hank? Mrs. Granger's name was on the printout; Joblobber's too. A Priddle may also be involved. He was seen entering the Futts's apartment. They're interrogating him. Indicates you've been acting strangely lately. *Guilty.* Mrs. Gribbley confirms this. Has supplied *other* evidence. Seems you were celebrating shortly after the incident, indulging in pornographic activities. Then, of course, we have your confession."

"*Confession.* Ridiculous! *Chocolates?* People are putting poison, pins, glass—all sorts of things—into...Maniacs. It doesn't mean—"

"To interrupt, Mr. Stickle. Is *this* ridiculous? Listen to Rod, my Pet."

"Kill my mother-in-law? It's alright. Of course I'm capable of the most terrible atrocities. I almost smashed a policeman's face today. Were it possible I'd of used bombs, anything to destroy people, property. I'm the perfect type to run concentration camps, cheer when the smoke pours from the chimneys..."

"Need I play more?"

"But where's the rest? It's all out of context. I denied *all* your accusations."

"I record only the important material, Mr. Stickle. The context is mine, not Rod's. Rather damning, wouldn't you say? Maybe you were in it with Futts. He's mentioned your name. And what of the rape of Mrs. Vanders, destruction of property in department stores, hurling snowballs—no doubt rock-filled—at officers. There are other things too, far worse. I must go, join Detective Fasten. You should contact him. He has questions."

"Rape! Futts. *In it?*...My place was burglarized, Detective Karaki. Guzman is going to tie a knot, I mean kill..."

"'...cheer when the smoke pours from the chimneys,' Mr. Stickle? Possibly you need a psychiatrist, institutionalization, quite likely incarceration. Your conspiracy with Guzman: I'd be careful, he's a dangerous associate. Very. We'll have some questions about Ramon—Mr. Echewy—later. Understand you took his job. Were you involved with that too? Hmmm. To enjoy. Ta ta."

"Won't you at least listen?..."

Vanished. Black slicing white through a slit in the wall. On the table behind where Karaki'd been sitting, a sheet, *body: Mums,* smiling, the coverlet pulled to her chin and folded back. Bedtime forever. The table moving on a track of some kind. Doors unfolding upwards from the floor, a ramp, the table disappearing. Speakers blaring:

"Croner, arrival on Runway Four. Party on hold."

A figure moving up the ramp, waving, floor closing.

"Gotta clean it up, H.S. Walkway Five there will get 'er out. Here Bart. Sit."

"Shumley?"

Jump suit, peak cap—all in white: a snowman with a tiny cart. Cart? No, coffin—vacuum?—striped black and white that rolled behind on wheel or rail.

"Moonlightin', Stickle. Can't make it do at the A.F. Gonna put in a 'lectric eye doodad soon: computer thing that do it all. Then that job be gone. May try the garbage. Say the pay there be good. Need the strong back, though. Ever think of workin' rubbish, H.S.?"

"No, I haven't, not yet anyway. Walkway Five?"

"She be up the end, 'round left."

"I don't see..."

"Show 'im Bart. *Pick a winner, not your nose!* 'Member that, H.S.? Good ole days. Seein' yuh."

Dog almost to his waist, eyes reddish, motor growling. On the left a slip-through space, then stairs, a door and street ahead.

"He down there, Stickle?"

"Who?...*Miz Fartlar.* Didn't see..."

"Apron missing too, Stickle. Stamper, apron. Crump, me—we want them back. Crime to steal. Snelly knows. Jail, Stickle; could mean that. I'd watch myself. Things can happen. *Bad* things."

Evening already? Morning when he'd arrived at Katzen-

116

bach's. Cars steaming, honking—a snaking blur that melted into buildings, purpling sky.

"Time, do you have?..."

"Two o'clock mister. Better get off the road, on the sidewalk. Drivers don't care. Soon's hit you as anything."

"Didn't realize...Thanks."

"You o'kay? Look kinda pale, sweatin'."

"No—yes, I'm fine, quite alright."

"Just askin'. Afternoon."

Suddenly the light poured down in milky shafts, a silvered moonlight poured through gauze. People slanting right and left with laugh and shout, the blare of horn and roar of subway underneath. Dizzy, spinning,must sit down. A bench ahead. Could that be Rostow at the lights? He'd make it home,then eat. That came first, and thinking next. There had to be a way. Survivor, winner—sure, why not?

The sky was clearing, chunks of blue. Karaki might have his Rod, but then again there was that other rod or staff mentioned in the Bible that was supposed to protect against enemies and evil: God's—that Being he could never imagine or really believe in. And if He did exist (maybe It was a She, a Mum Granger writ large), how would that entity think of Horace Stickle?: as a soul in need of rewiring, a new program? —perhaps a sound thrashing with God-Person's cane or walking stick?

For now, his best hope was probly to keep his fingers crossed and knock on wood. Damn, the bench was cement. So what? Always darkest before the dawn, they said. The sky had been black a few minutes ago, and now the day was radiant. He couldn't lose, he just couldn't.

Bells ringing, crowds cheering to the raising of the lid. He had survived the river of fire in his midget submarine, but...Sealed in again, the top screwed down and darkness back. No heat this time, the ringing faint and cheering gone. Cold crept in and water too: a slime that rose to chest and nose. A final thrust, a shout, then light and voices just in time.

"Is that Mr. Stickle? Mr. Stickle, are you alright?"

117

"Who is this, where?..."

Home? The bench...Window open, feet resting on a heating duct, a voice beneath him somewhere on the couch. Phone, receiver off...

"Hello, Stickle speaking. Fine, I'm here, at the phone. Who is this please?"

"Grunulda Moloch, Mr. Stickle. We've met twice, I believe."

*"Mrs. Moloch?...*are you sure?—me?...to speak?..."

"Mr. Stickle, I understand you've had, shall we say, a job problem. Perhaps I could help. Would you care to drop over about eight?"

"Yes, of course. Why would you take an interest? I mean..."

"Suffice to say, Mr. Stickle, I'm fascinated by elk—you'll recall those photographs my husband mentioned last night. We can discuss them later. One, Old Mellow Road is the address. Good evening, Mr. Stickle."

Would Moloch be there? Maybe a last chance to reason with him, find out more about Guzman. Moloch seemed in trouble with the man too. On the other hand...

Seven o'clock. Must've fallen asleep when he got home. Snow drifting through a broken pane; a healing white to bandage up the ravaged room, his throbbing head. Elk and photos, loose ends, knots. Words, like snowflakes (people?), sifting by, their meaning melting fast, then gone. Would that be his fate?: a speck of water, empty space...Come to think of it, that was better than a pool of blood, preferable by far to the gun and rope others seemed anxious to inflict on him. But best of all was somehow to see daylight, spot Shumley in the clear and throw a pass, connect for once, score a touchdown, the winning one.

*   .

"Mrs. Moloch?"

"Come in. Tremor knocked out the power this morning. Still not fixed. Had to make do with candles. This way, please."

"Mrs. Moloch, I'm afraid none of this makes any sense."

"We're all afraid, Mr. Stickle. Too much sense, one gets suspicious, feels persecuted; too little and we throw up our hands. We must hold fast, be men, not mice. Yes yes yes?"

118

"I wouldn't go so far…"

The woman, gangling, a network of branches in the flickering light. Mice: the damn rodents would follow him to the grave.

"Here will be fine. Candles a bit closer, there. Now…"

"Mr. Moloch…*Mrs.* Moloch, I thought he—your husband—would be…I wouldn't want him to find…"

"Wednesdays are always late, Mr. Stickle. The *visit* will have him busy till all hours. Now, I presume the Thurmond people arranged it from—To excuse, a drink?"

"No, I don't…"

"Join me in a scotch, Mr. Stickle. Troubles, these shocks, need lubrication to ease the…*strain* might be the *mot juste.*"

"Thank you, I guess one…"

She crossed the room in a fluid lope and disappeared. Something streaked past his foot, around the couch and into shadow.

"Here we are, Mr. Stickle. Cheers. May we continue? The agency was *très* clever in employing an inside man for the operation. Indeed, indeed."

"Mrs.—"

"Ta ta. But the elk is mine, my good man. Paid for in full. It would seem you are, as they say, trying to have your moose, elk, whatever, and eat it too. Playing both sides of the kazoo, speaking with the double mouth."

"Mrs.…."

She wasn't listening, draining Scotch. How much had she poured? Large tumblers, no mix or ice. A fleeting form cut to his left.

"The point is, Mr. Stickle, I don't want revenge, not at all. Justice is mine, saith the Lord. It belongs to me too, also you, Mr. Stickle. Fair enough?"

"Mrs. Stickle—Moloch—I cannot understand…"

"With knowledge cometh understanding, Mr. Stickle, and thus followeth wisdom. It's in the Bible."

"I'm sure, but…"

"Drink up, jolly man. You're a little behind. Can't have that, can we? Oh I should say not. You might pour, this time. Behind us on the service, by the candelabra."

The bottle awkward, heavy. Tumblers brimming. "Here you are Mrs.—whoops." Something brushing ankle, foot, then

119

gone. "Sorry, spilled…My handkerchief, here let me wipe…"

Fingers curling firmly round his wrist, his hand rising, drawn steadily away from her skirt and thigh.

"In the *wash,* Mr. Stickle. Later."

"Sorry, I…"

Had he been rubbing?…

"Quite alright, Mr.—Is it Horace? Under other circumstances, I might find your advances—ambiance?—stimulating. But then I do not play games. Maddox is the expert in that department. Oh, I'll say he is."

Stimulating? Had a woman ever told him that, even Ethel? He'd explain everything…

"Mrs. Moloch—"

"Grunulda."

"Yes…Grun, Grunulda. First they computerized—"

"My dear little man, I have your file, your life, in my lap. What I lack is your connection with Thurmond, the agency."

"Mrs.…Grunulda, I've never heard of them. Mr. Moloch fired me last night. When I opened the other bathroom door yesterday, he was furious. Then he talked of photographs at the elevator, seemed friendly. I…" ·

"*Other* bathroom door?"

"Yes, I…after the cart spilled…very nervous. I had to go…Sure, I knew it wasn't proper to use his private one. But to fire me after twenty-five years…I—"

"*Furious,* you say? Was there any *other* reason? I must know, Mr.—Horace. He wants to cut me off without a cent. Dump me for his little pretties. He can do it, Horace. He has all the money, lawyers. Doesn't find me attractive now. The accident, you know: Maddox not a scratch. But it was a glass eye for me, new teeth, other problems. I feel at times like experimental art: a—a happening. Was there anything else?…"

"No, not really. He was with Miss Cuddy, talking. I didn't listen—"

"*Cuddy?* She was with Maddox, in this *other* room? I've been through his office. There is no—"

"Yes, Miss Cuddy. She was…My eyes haven't been working too well…"

An affair. Was that?…More connections missed, melon asleep, misfiring. Maybe it *had* been a garter belt. But then

120

was he any better? What about Manny's? "I'm sorry, Mrs.—"

"Doubtless Maddox wasn't. Too bad the coffee wagon didn't all land in his lap. Shame there were no photographs. Maddox must have realized that last night, knows you're not with Thurmond. Your word against his. Useless in court. Being fired, they'd presume revenge on your part anyway. Maybe Thurmond can catch...Well, that's another day, is it not?"

"I'm not interested in getting even, Mrs.—Grunulda. Just, a glimpse of sky, an equation where...Better be off..."

"One more thing, Horace: You spoke of a Guzman and Katzenbach last night. The agency gave me this tape. Hooked it to our phone some way. Those names—also a K—and others are mentioned, Schwingalt too, plus a Strum or Strun. Strange conversations. They...something unsettling about them. I really don't want to learn more. Take it. What's said might help pressure Maddox about your job. You don't seem the type, though, that would be involved."

"I'm not, but somehow I am. Guzman thinks... Time to leave, Mrs. Moloch—Grunulda."

"One more. For luck?"

"Yes, that would be fine. Luck, a drink—both I mean."

Her face ageless in the candles' flicker: Indian, an ancient mask, the right eye fixed and gleaming, luminous in the dark.

A whining hiss, then needles stabbing neck and scalp. Stumbling, falling toward the couch, across her lap, the liquor spilling, tape airborn.

"Mr.—Precious, it was..."

Struggling to sit up. Grunulda bending down, his arms somehow around her neck, then tight together, kissing, pulling...A flash of light.

"That will be all, Striker. Keep the negative. Send me the photos.

"I thought it was women, dear. But I see your corruption works both ways. Alcohol, orgy—truly the Devil's work."

"You'd be an expert on that, Maddox."

"What the?...*Precious.* The poor cat is distraught! Stickle, if you've hurt her, I'll have you arrested, jailed. Come here, sweetheart."

"Mr. Moloch, I do not apologize for kissing your wife. It

121

isn't what you think. There are kisses and *kisses*. Didn't you ever hug your mother, kiss her?"

"You can talk about that in court, Stickle. Convince a jury my wife is your mother. That you're not an adulterer, have made me a cuckhold."

"Mr. Moloch, there are things I know, heard today. You could be in trouble..."

"Yes, we know. Guzman picked you up on video, spying. Only your word, Stickle, the word of a disgruntled employee: a snoop, incompetent, a moral leper. Besides, the conversation was in code, pertained to matters of security. Guzman is annoyed, very. I wouldn't say anything. Quiet, shh—like a mouse, a dead one if you're not careful."

"Mouse. Look here—"

"Striker, show him out."

"Goodnight, Mrs.—Grunulda."

"Thank you, Horace, for your help. I have no apologies either. Hi ho. Merry Christmas."

Grunulda, face now softer (almost pretty?) in the wavering candlelight, a human spark that lit the night. While Moloch shadowed near the door was more the cat that arched and writhed with hissing wrath against his shin.

Shouldn't have had so much Scotch. The warming tug was now a fist that blossomed redly in his head. The ping and whir of elevators came from up ahead. He stumbled, dizzy, reaching out to hold the door and grabbed a woman just inside.

"What do you think you're!...Let *go* before I call..."

The face familiar, blurring...must sit down. Legs out-stretched, his back against the elevator wall.

"Miss Cuddy?...Is it?..."

"Who?—I've seen you...Cart Man...I..."

"It's, Horace, the name is..."

"Are you alright? Here, let me help you up. My floor, we're almost...There, I'll hold the door. The apartment—this one on the left. A glass of water perhaps."

"Thank you, not really necessary. I..."

Then inside and sitting down, drink of soda in his hand.

"A doctor, are you sure you don't want?..."

"Yes, I...really have to go..."

On his feet again, her arm about his shoulder, steadying

122

him. The clink of key, a figure looming at the door.

"Pumpkin, sweet. I—who is!...You!..."

"Mr. Moloch...Evening, Miss Cuddy. Must be going, I really must...Thank you..."

*

The night rushed toward him on the street, its silver headlight bearing down: a frozen train from long lost time whose windows twinkled in the dark. Strange images again that swept him up and dropped him in another place.

"Waiting for doomsday, Stickle? Plan to roost in the hallway. Guess it's better'n that hog-pen in your place."

"Mrs. Gribbley. Didn't realize I was sitting..."

"No small wonder. Smell the liquor from here. Better shape up, take a good look at yourself. Blind, that's what you are. Don't see nothin'. 'Member what happened to the mice, Stickle: got their tails sliced with the carving knife. Wouldn't doubt that's what's gonna happen to you. The wife or someone will oblige. Your missus don't look none too happy these days."

"Mrs. Gribbley...Merry Christmas, happy—"

"Nothin' merry 'bout it, Stickle. Time when the real greedies come outer their holes. Here, I brung you this book: *Hellfire for Men.* Changed Fred's whole life. Never can tell, might even turn somethin' like you 'round. By Great Gran Mums Gribbley when she was ninety—*Ninety,* mind you. An inspiration if'n there ever was."

"Thank you—"

"No thanks, Stickle. Read, memorize it. Mightn't get so hot for yuh later."

He was inside at last where TV glowed across the room. A face, mask, slipped off the screen, rose up and floated round his head, then grinning spun back to the set. Hands chucked papers, music blared and dazzling teeth chopped rapid words: "...Time for our late sports roundup, all you night riders out in Never Never Land." Vibrant chuckle, wink and wave. "There were several hockey games..."

Games. Hadn't that man Tilvnit, or whatever, the other night at Harbor View asked him about *his* game? Maybe he was out of it already, in the penalty box, suspended. Could that be what life was all about?: a carnival of midway madness to see who could win the most prizes, friends to influence, stuffed animals and other things; something winnable at the expense of others, even oneself, one's own life, the world even, in the ultimate game of nuclear war? There had to be more than that...than perhaps Amalgamated, something that added to himself, gave him size—yes, those sails that skimmed the foam, one good, clean memory he could ride into eternity. A feeling, instinct that might help him keep the faith, believe— what?— that perhaps goodness, not the blackness, would prevail?

"...And in the Gardens, a free-for-all broke out in the third period after Rambolt's vicious cross-check on Bunns. A real kamikaze. Several fans and players were hospitalized. Stupa-vitch, who was brutally sticked in the face by Grinch, required one hundred and thirty stitches..."

Looked as if the police in the film clip were waving guns. There, near the back of the arena, a spectator running with a rifle? Pools of blood on the rink, closeups of teeth splattered...

"Pig-Out. A Mr. Stickle. Pig-Out."

"Sorry, no order. I didn't!..."

"QUIET STICKLE!"

"PIG-OUT!"

"NOT ME, MRS. GRIBBLEY."

"THAT YOU H.S.? STINKY HERE. OPEN 'ER UP. GOTCH YOUR SANICH, MONSTER."

"Shumley? What?...Come in. I didn't order—"

"Shhh. Listen. The telly. Talking 'bout him now."

"...And President Ralpher's strategy enunciated at his news conference was to conduct war games off the coast, military exercises on shore. The carriers involved contain enough fire power to obliterate all the countries in the area. Government forces of junta leader Generalissimo Barte supported by this country are reported to have eliminated over forty thousand men, women and children who were considered subversive in backing the rebels' People's Party. President Ralpher empha-sized again that we can ill afford the violence of a People's Marxist-Leninist dictatorship regime on our very doorstep, that the issue is directly one of Good versus Evil."

"Right, he be, eh, H.S.? Things is movin'. Why—"

124

"SHUMLEY, YOU IN THERE?"

"QUIET, I SAY..."

"That be the Missus callin', H.S. She there in the hallway, walkin' Barty. Gotta be gettin' 'er on out now. Here's your— Ain't that a ripper? Your sanich, it be all gone. Old Stinky, he ate the whole thing. Hmmm. We's closin' in, though, H.S., evenin' the score soon. Oh you betcha. Pass the word. Ciao."

What word? Whose?: God's, the Devil's?—Shumley's, perhaps his own? And what would that be?: that no one seemed to speak the truth, let alone Truth. What was it the Indians had always said about the White Man?: that he spoke with forked tongue, his words twisted, their meaning gnarled and foreign like the branches clawing moonlight beyond the windowpane. Maybe today, though, it was more the lying to oneself, yes, the treaties he, Horace Stickle, had broken to himself, that mattered. But damn it, about what, which promises? That was the problem, the touch of bat and nibble of mouse that bothered him.

From the hallway, growling, thunder rising to a belching roar—the dog, it must be...

"SHUT UP, STICKLE! THE POLICE, I'LL CALL THEM! I'LL—"

"IT'S BART, MRS.—"

"HELL AWAITS YOU, WRETCHED MAN! READ GRAN MUMS, GO READ THE WORD. IT'S IN THE BOOK!"

Scarlet flares mushroomed on the TV and moved inside his head to the crash of military music. And after sound and color faded from the set, he addressed the world as Super Mouse, while planetary crowds that thronged horizons anthemned forth their praise.

Later in another dream he stumbled shaking, cold and wet down inky holes and lost his way. "The game is ending, almost over over over...," came the chant, a booming throb from heart to head. But not quite yet, no not that night.

12

ODD, COULDN'T sit up. Numb, cold, the stench of pizza at his head. Was it day or night? More a twilight drifting past with formless shapes, the edges blurred. A voice, that roaring... "CATSPAW HUGGINS HERE, ALL YOU EARLY MORNIN' PEAPICKERS, WITH *I AINT DEAD YET FRED.* TICKLE THAT CATGUT—"

"We interrupt programming at this time for our regular newsbreak special: Flash Stud of Rolling Crud was found hanging in his closet early this morning. Police suspect foul play."

On the floor, he was...Must've slipped off the couch, fallen onto the pizza...

"...Limited nuclear war, I repeat, only *limited* war, has broken out in the regions mentioned in our last report. There has been no comment from President Ralpher who is ending a vacation out West to visit Amalgamated.

"Developments as they occur on the Crud situation.

"Now back to your breakfast music for Lovers Only."

"...AH WANTA BE YOAH SLAVE, FRED, UNTIL YOAH DEAD DEAD DEAD, FRED..."

"LAST TIME, STICKLE: THE NOISE—SHUT THE SOUND. DEVIL'S PLAYGROUND..."

There, off. The President visiting Amalgamated?: heard something about it over the intercom the other day, hadn't he? Could that be the answer?—Ralpher? Somehow say something to him?...Impossible. No way to get through...What to tell him, if he could?: that there might be hundreds, maybe millions of people in his shoes—the now empty oxfords of Horace Stickle—being replaced, turfed out of work with really nowhere to go, nowhere that made too much sense. Sure, there were the *Apples* and *Pets*—hadn't really given them much of a chance. Maybe later, in different circumstances. For now, the Stickle he'd imagined, longed to catch, was becoming someone, something else: maybe the man who'd turned away in the mirror: perhaps even the mirror itself changing reflections—magic, a new funhouse he couldn't navigate. The President, though, should know, be told by someone involved what it was like: the taste of pennies, slippery hands—yes, the feeling of tiny feet running up and down one's spine.

"Now our gospel thought for the hour, friends and neighbors, your favorite and mine. Father Love."

"FATHER LOVE, HERE. I SAY HATE THE DEVIL, ALL YOU SINNERS, LOATHE THAT LITTLE BOOGER, THAT SLIMY CRITTER. HE EVERYWHERE: IN YOU, ME, IN ALL OF US. TAKE AWAY THE 'D' YOU HAVE 'EVIL.' THE DEVIL IS EVIL, MY GOOD FRIENDS..."

"THAT'S IT, STICKLE. CALLIN' THE SIRENS, RED LIGHTS."

"She went to London to visit the queen, Mrs. Gribbley! I'm going to Amalgamated to talk to the President. You'll see: Foch will fix my head, I'll get through...I own a share in Company, a vote. I have a right to be heard..."

"NO RIGHTS IN JAIL. DO TIME, STICKLE. YOU NEED TIME."

That cord snaking from the pile of clothes. Yank...harder. So much for the radio. Dizzy. Lie on the floor. Phone beside him. An appointment...

"Doctor Foch, please."

"Yo."

"Doctor Foch?"

128

"Yo."

"This is Horace Stickle. You arranged...Doctor Groat, my head...I'm not officially terminated. No pink slip yet. I can still use Company's medical..."

Damn tongue glued to the roof of his mouth.

"Can't hear you, son. Pickle, you're in a pickle, you say? Not dead yet, eh? Neither am I. Your goat—the vet takes care—"

"No Groat! Doctor Groat, I, you..."

"Foch here. Groat is elsewhere."

"Doctor..."

"Stickle, is it? Recognize the voice. Yes, be here within the hour. We need to recheck the ole pizzerello. Ciao."

The gloom outside was lifting slightly, now streaked through with bluish white. He'd feel better on the street. Cold air would clear his head, sharpen focus. Outlook—that was the thing. Just hard to find the proper one, sometimes any at all.

"Nurse, my name is Horace Stickle. I have an appointment— Dr. Foch..."

"Let me check...Sorry blinking red, it's—"

"'Scuse Nurse, 'mergency! Names Shumley. It's Ralph there, down below. Needs the Doc. Like as not gas, the vapors again. Yellin', laughin', runnin'...Dee doo, there, H.S.... What brings? —Here come Doc now..."

"Nurse—ah Stickle, just reviewing your—"

"I'm Shumley, Doc; he be Stickle. Trouble down there below: Ralph. Fit or sumpin'. Chute Ten."

"That'd be basement, of course. Bone, Ralph: examined him last week. Blind, isn't he, partially deaf? Hmmm. Falling to pieces, I believe. This way, we'll go express. Tap the coconut later, Mr. Stickle. Chi Chi."

"Nurse, is there any other doctor? Head, very..."

"Sorry, Mr. Shumley, flashing red, we have a red. I must go. Later, check back then."

"The name's, Stickle, Nurse. What time should—"

"Out of the way, please! Let the stretcher through!"

"Sorry..."

The patient wheezing, face doughy with bulging eyes. He seemed familiar...Another man in overalls behind the litter, grinning, holding a wrench, extending his hand. "Swallowed a bone, so's I hear. You Foch?"

"No, no I'm Stickle, Horace..."

"Name's Bone, Ralph Bone. Sticks in my craw too. Ha ha."

"I believe Doctor Foch went with Shumley to—"

"Shumley? Man's crazier than a coot. Ha! Where's Bart? Here boy. Come get yer Bone. Ho. Oh ain't it grand, Doctor Foch, just ginger peachy?"

Head starting to whirl, a pinball machine revving up. And the squealing in his stomach reminded him of beasties he'd sooner forget. While waiting, he'd go upstairs, check the executive coffee room. Must've left his suitcoat there the other day. Maybe he could find out something about Ralpher's visit too. There was always a chance...

13

"MISS CUDDY, good morning—afternoon. I—"

"Cart Boy! Thank goodness you're here! They're expected any minute. Stoneball's gone, choked on something he was tasting. Here, this is his clearance badge. That man in the black suit will let you through. I was to see everything went smoothly for the luncheon. Mr. Moloch will be furious. Hurry...the food, your uniform—let me show you. Down here."

"Miss Cuddy, I can't handle—serve a luncheon. I haven't the faintest idea...Not feeling—"

"But it's the President—what's his name—and that Russian man. Other important people too."

"President. You mean he's?—"

"Yes, and the Russian: Gorshit, or something. The visit wasn't supposed to be today. They changed it: security reasons, I think. Mr. Moloch is terribly upset. Came in late. I'll help, do anything. Please Mr?..."

"Stickle. I'll try, Miss Cuddy, do whatever..."

"You're a darling. For luck."

A kiss, brushing of the cheek? So much better than Susy-Q and other such things. Buzzer already? One long, a short.

"That's Mr. Moloch for service, Mr. Stickle. Is there anything?..."

"This meal-machine is a lot different than the coffee wagon, Miss Cuddy. The control panel on the handle is confusing: dials, switches, levers. You say Stoneball has everything ready inside? I hope so..."

Blasted contraption resembled a miniature spacecraft with rocket boosters flanking the main cylinder. Problem was, Commander Stickle didn't have his wings, couldn't fly a kite.

"There it is again, Mr. Stickle: red blinker and buzzer. Means immediately. Forget the tuxedo. Your sportscoat—stains on the lapel...Those swinging doors are to the dining room, they open automatically when you get near. *Watch out...*"

Through the entrance...rolling too quickly...pull back. Hadn't he pressed?...No, the "Fast" button beside "Go" was blinking. Better hit "Slow." Why had it stopped? Low humming from the instrument panel. Moloch on his feet, speaking. Hadn't spotted him yet in the alcove.

"...And so, Mr. President, Premier Gorshev, honored guests, during luncheon we will attempt to show you in part how the headquarters of a large multinational conglomerate, the economic centerpiece of our democratic system, keeps abreast of its foreign and domestic operations..."

Moloch, a shaft of black with pate aglow. Hands blocking, chopping, fanning air. A dream, someone else's. He didn't belong, was trespassing. *Speak* to the President?—had he really intended?...

"...The key element is information technology, the global linkage of communications and computer technology that accesses headquarters to immediate information. Audio-visual teleconferencing—'In-House', 'Out-House'—through the several monitor screens on the wall enables face-to-face meetings with foreign, domestic, and headquarters' executives to be arranged almost instantly, thus facilitating coordination and implementation of decision-making processes. We..."

Decisions. Did he really dare approach, Ralpher? They could...*They?* What could they *really* do?—shoot?...maybe arrest?...Prison, locks....*DO TIME, STICKLE, YOU NEED TIME...* Warden Gribbley...

"...The twenty-ninth floor of A.F., where we are gathered, is in a way a cosmological principle, a guiding beacon in the darkest night, if you will, to our far-flung empire. The lines of communication are always open, the fingers of the executive committee, myself, directors, always on the pulse of our business, sensitive to the weather of our competition, the storms in the night, the sunrises that bless with profit. Just as man proposes and God disposes, so do I—we here—with His help similarily communicate with them—officers—out there. All sides of a problem or venture are judiciously considered by us; and then the Word goes forth in the twinkling of an eye that *they* may execute as appropriate. Yet—"

"True democracy in action, is it not, Mr. Moloch?"

"Mr. President?"

"Everybody has his say, then *you* decide, slice the pie. Let them know immediately if it's *à la mode* or whatever?"

"Indeed, Mr. President, you're quite right. I run a tight ship, let me assure you. Have consultants trimming sails, battening down hatches. It may be a two way street; but I operate the intersections, traffic lights."

"Good, Mr. Moloch. Can't have the system run like a Sunday school picnic: everybody sorta steppin' on the other fellow's plate. Ride a horse, you hold the reins. Like as not end up on a cow patty, if you don't. Heh."

"To be sure, Mr. President. With our reins, that is to say the revolution in communications and information processing, we at headquarters can better ensure that the A.F. policies—culture or principles, if you will—are imposed on all our corporate family to ensure synchronization and standardization in the pursuit—"

"Zat is vut vee do vit der Party and State, Mr. Mulluck: kip der kintrul for zee pipples. Frum itch accordink hiss ahbiltee, to itch hiss need. Luk der Goldun Rull in yur Bibble. All vee do is force der pipples ohbay der Rull, share der propurty. After ull, eet belung to zem anyvay. Iss zat zee revoushun you haff? Vut is so vunderful 'bout zat? Iss notink 'riginal, nyet?"

Gorshev, a massive cube with metal teeth that glinted dully through the beard, hunched forward. Was he looking at him? Why had the Premier grabbed a fork and jabbed it in his direction? Maybe he wanted food, drink.

133

"Excellent question, Premier Gorshev. I'd like to turn it over to my close associate, Mr. Schwingalt, our senior vice-president in charge of Resource Planning. Mr. Schwingalt."

"Iss Shvingult, not *Strum?* To say...nyet. I lissun."

"Yes, it's Schwingalt, Mr. Premier. Mr. Moloch meant to say, I'm sure, that my function is primarily in the area of financial planning, *money.* However, I understand Vice President Furly, head of our Research and Development Department, is about to demonstrate artificial intelligence in the service of our luncheon. I think he could furnish the best answer to the Premier's question."

Someone tapping him on the shoulder, pointing to the dining area. They must want service now. Press "Slow." Good, moving ahead—no, turning around, moving backwards...

"Stickle, Mr....you!...Why isn't Furly, Mr. Furly?..."

Heads turning toward him. Moloch on his feet. All of them tiny, insects viewed from the wrong end of a telescope. His chance, now..."President Ralpher, I would like to just say—"

"Whackenberry here, Maddox. Message you called."

"Lorimer! What?...Is this a joke? Will you please get off monitor. Furly's going to demonstrate...Excuse, ladies and gentlemen, this is the 'In-House' system I was referring to. That is Mr. Whackenberry. Now we can see each other, confer. But he is no longer with—"

"I'm not gone at all, Maddox, just between the grids. Am I coming through? Good. Furly's at East with Rumwalt. They're in transit. Now—"

"East! Rumwalt closed that operation—"

"Moved it North as agreed, Maddox. The fire, heat loss, you know. But we had insurance, fresh information. It's a new play with added drama, different sets. We have hot relationships, loaded grapevines. People jumping out of cakes. Yes indeed. Now what's the problem? Make it quick. I have a doctor's appointment. Those damn hemorrhoids."

"Lorimer, the problem!...Could you please briefly define for Premier Gorshev?— You *can* see President Ralpher and Gor—Premier Gorshev, can you not?"

"Distance isn't working. Can only see your legs, Maddox. Not a pretty sight. Hah!"

"They're here, Lorimer, *upstairs* at the luncheon. Surely you heard...Now—"

"Well, Rolf, the new cart, is in design downstairs! Vice-President Hanglingler—Counterintelligence—would be your man. The headspar short-circuited a 'Z' wire or something, and the on-board computer needs a fit. We require more information and 'F' chips from Rumwalt. Serve on Murray. Ramon used it. He's on special assignment now."

"Yes, Lorimer. Perhaps you could answer the Premier's question. He—it's fine to begin serving, Mr. Stickle—wants to know, get a background on this revolution, the information thing, syndrome."

Blasted machine had him pinned to the wall. "Stop" button not working, the wagon still purring away in reverse. Try that blinking red...A small drawer sliding... *Gun!*—Ramon's?...Put it in his pocket, they mustn't see...

"Have a tape on your information query, Maddox. Playing it now. Video East is in progress. I'm needed. Later, I'll be back then."

"We can't see you, Lorimer. Those pipes...Whackenberry, the tape—you have a movie!..."

"Hello, I'm Strange Sam..."

"I'm sorry ladies and...Maybe this dial."

"...To continue, the revolution, the third, following the agricultural and industrial, involves the organization and structuring of the information explosion—pollution—through modern computer and communication systems to create usable knowledge—information that is current, accurate and quickly accessible..."

"Mr. Stickle, you may initiate service now! Lorimer... Whackenberry! On screen, that animal—"

"Dot iss un dug, Mr. Mohluck. I vish to hear more—" *Bart! come!..."*

"Der Burt iss not huss brukin. Luk, ull ovur der flur."

"...In an increasingly diverse, but interdependent world, such knowledge is not just a mere aid to solving problems and maintaining a workable integration, but a key resource, a new property, for meeting needs on every level of society, indeed, for preserving our survival in the nuclear era. We..."

"High-Tech on Monitor Three—Domestic West: This is a recorded announcement. We are under 'Red Eye' alert. Incoming missile systems have been tracked. Incomplete data, defective circuit breakers. To repeat, until further notice, this has been a recorded..."

"Crowling on Monitor Chips. Sorry about that blip, Maddox. Just "gaming." In the middle of a changeover. What's up?"

"Weren't you notified, Crowling, that?—Ladies and gentlemen, Mr. Fumgate Crowling is president of our High-Tech Division. He—"

"Haven't been advised of anything from your end, Mad. Just got in from the Orient. Carlo is walking the ceiling. Two of his boys got nabbed for allegedly stealing classified information from the Hiroshito people on the 'sixty-four' byte question—hah, no pun intended. A real stink. Ought to be on the wire at your end soon. They've implicated Carl-baby. Say it was his idea. Apparently Carl is pointing the finger at headquarters."

"Headquarters! Not?—"

"Already named you, Schwingalt, Schoner. Says he has replays from tapes, claims that you specifically ordered—"

"Crowling, the President, Premier—"

"...Knowledge is becoming society's most valuable and powerful form of property: the New Wealth, force of production that will revolutionize society, consciousness, and which even now is the fuel that drives two thirds of our economy. It is not just a renewable resource as opposed to non renewable, it is expandable through distribution and use. For instance..."

"Gut Got, Mr. Moluck, vut is dis?...in my lap, *shrimpzees*?"

"Terribly sorry, Premier Gorshev."

"Stick...Mr. Stickle, this *isn't* Murray, the regular dining car!"

"Mr. Moloch, I have no idea...I'm doing...it's a *favor* to Miss Cuddy...President Ralpher, if I might have a moment—"

"Hanglinger here, Maddox, Horace. Yes, on 'In-House.' That's Bruce, the other experimental model. Murray is down for repairs: a broken collateral. Boo-Boo is remote and also voice controlled. The panel is removable, can be worked from the alcove. Speak the designated instructions, if you wish. Talk to Bruce."

"Where's Whacken...*Hanglinger!* What!..."

"Hear, but can't see you, Maddox. Am I voiced in? The new force is going South. I'm changing zones. The renovated complex is lasered."

"What are you talking?...Hanglinger? Gone. Must be the programming. He passed away several..."

"Well, I've never...That thing pinched...Stop it immediately!"

"Mrs. Ralpher, what?..."

136

"Disgusting thing squeezed…Dress ruined, gravy, sauce…"

"I am Bruce. Watch me serve."

"Whackenberry back. Command pincer to move left, right, forward, back, as appropriate. Punch 'Appetizer', then 'Meal'; follow with 'Dessert.' TV eyes on the cannister ends will do the rest. I have to go. Buttocks—very painful. Lost my donut, the little cushion."

"Excuse, Mr. Whackenberry. A moment. Horace Stickle here. Your voice has activated the cart. Could you please neutralize?…"

The sound system must have failed. No response. Whackenberry's mouth still moving, head upside down on the screen. Was that Miz Fartlar behind him? Earl Battle by the pipes?

Blasted cart gyrating spastically, rod-like extensions with pincer-grips tweaking at people, pushing food: a steak in Moloch's lap, fruit cup dribbling over the President's shoes. Remove panel? Hanglinger'd said it came off. There, maybe he could work it on remote control from the alcove. At this rate he'd never get to the President.

"…Know why I'm called Strange?…"

"…The implications of the revolution's impact on economic theory, legal concepts, business management, social and political systems will require some fundamental rethinking…"

"Lorimer, the 'Volume' dial!: the voice is too loud!"

"Bruce likes to serve fine folks the very best."

"Maddox, the scrambler has been activated at your end. You're garbled."

"Audio poor, Lorimer, I can't hear…Now it's coming…"

"Mr. Stickle, Bruce is shoving the table; could you reverse? …"

"Bruce now serves desserts."

"…Production of knowledge and information gives rise to sharing rather than exchange transactions indicative of both capitalist and socialist economic systems and will require those systems' conceptions of property to be somewhat transformed. I give or sell you a piece of cake; you have it and I don't; I give or sell you information and we both have it. So you see…"

"Mr. President, you wished to say?…"

"Mr. Moloch, we've sorta tried that *sharing* business before with our welfare programs. Doesn't work. Socialistic, stifles entrepreneurship and—If you please, Cart, Bruce—fellah, whatever—not the ice cream now! Later, I'll have it…The

Tin Lizzy is shoving...Waiter, could you?..."

"...In my lap, spilled all over!..."

"Presdunt Rulfer, der mun vit kuntrul panul, he doss not unterstand zis Whuckyburry, nyet? Ziss new system, she not vurk, yah? Zay sharink zee akurat eenformashun, vut vee dunt get der fud. Hah."

"Mr. Stickle, by hand will be sufficient. If you will just get Mr. Stoneball..."

"That's not possible, Mr. Moloch, he swallowed a bone, and...Mr. President—"

"Iss Stonebull zat dug vee saw on der scrin?"

"No, Mr. Premier, he's—"

"That you, Stickle? Lorimer here. Welcome aboard. Corn's popping, butter's hot. You'll be hearing."

Hearing? Yes, there it was, the roaring of waterfalls, now receding to a whisper, then growing rapidly louder, insistent, to jackhammer pounding that...And in the background, a steady beat, more words, the metronome of the tape, other voices flowing...

"...And in a world of shared resources...relations...gravitate to new levels of cooperation...humanistic competition rather than adversarial... Information...should encourage maximization of choice...not suppression of diversity..."

"Crowling again, Maddox. Just in—bit of a poop. Those test robots—the ones to replace conventional troops—they killed some regular soldiers in the pilot maneuver: head circuits—it seems an 'F' wire crossed..."

"I am Bruce, watch me..."

"Want to know why Shirly is Strange?..."

"Whackenberry, get that movie off!..."

"...In a world with nobody in charge, but everybody partly in charge, collegial rather than command structures are the natural basis for organization; the trend also being to a more sensitive and caring style of management and society that..."

"A question, Mr. President?"

"Yes, Mr. Moloch. Sounds like an evangelical revival. You spoke earlier of central control—all that standardization stuff. This Whacken whatever tape—it doesn't jibe: speaks of everyone thumbing the pie. Who really cares, is responsible for the black ink, bottom line?: God, or the Chairman of the Board?"

Certain words struck a chord. Body trembling; even his head, the old melon, seemed to quiver. A voice—his?—hollow, thin. *"Care? Caring? Who really does care, Mr. President? Who? Do you?"*

Why were they staring at him, motionless, forks poised in mid air. The gun—magic—suddenly in his hand, a tiny toy. Slight movement to his left—the machine, tentacles pawing, groping. Ralpher, rising slowly, talking.

"Well, my good man, and you might be?..."

"Stickle, Horace Stickle—H.S. for short. I just wanted to say—"

"Yes yes, by all means. But first...That *gun,* we don't need—"

"Mr. President, have you ever felt tiny feet, mice if you will—"

"That you, Maddox? Schoner here on Monitor Two. Outside counsel advises several divisions legally bankrupt and—"

The voice had surprised him. Had the gun fired? Schoner was gone, screen too, but...Ralpher—a mummy's face in blue-white glare, the hair a shock of black swept back, a ruby pucker at the lips—was talking quickly now. His voice a whisper, confident, and then a growling baritone while hands chopped points, and hair, a living mass, rose higher, mounding, flowing as he spoke.

"...My fellow Americans, Mr. Stinkle, may I say with deepest conviction that I care, we all care. Do you not know that the game plan, the big one, life, is one of profit based on ability and virtue, the greatest virtue being love, the capacity to care for your adversary, the competitor whose money you want? Do you not realize that this struggle—Warfare System, if you want—for the fruits of success, is the price,the retail cost of our democratic system? For profit and liberty are, so-to-speak, Siamese twins. Yes, we are really only free, equal— in a way immortal—when we have enough in the bank— affluence —to pursue our highest ideal: to fully realize our net worth and invest it in the production of happiness, that ultimate factory of the free enterprise system—"

"Horace! What in heaven's name?...This is Ethel, Monitor Five..."

Ethel, frowning, her face a crosshatched blur. Was that a whip in her hand?—microphone, cord? Pain—a sizzling red behind the eyes. Silver glint, a pincer's grab that brushed his nose.

"Whackenberry here. Emergency in the silo. Must go, Maddox. Good work, Horace. Hold the fort."

"...Mugabe, Horace! Remember what I told you...Amin..."

Her face dissolving, black line, gone. Then squirming coils, a grid, another face.

"Henry—Harriet here, dear—uh, Horace, Mr. Stickle. The kiss, it didn't matter, you mustn't...This isn't the way to soldier, fight. You must..."

"Fight!" Had he yelled? Voice, a belling in his ears. Fight what, though?—oppression, injustice...the System? Seemed impossible. Maybe that's why people fought each other—easier, the adversary clear, *there,* not concealed. To win, succeed, was money, power—Ralpher's algebra of kill and love. Then the jackpot—"happy hour"—planting crops with Mugabe. Utopias on every lip, the Golden City in the mist, so far, so close, yet never reached. He needed words—better still the Word, a feeling, sign, something...Sweat, rivers...even his socks, wet, slippery...His voice, faint, distant. "Mice, we are not—"

"'Cheer when the smoke goes up the chimney,' Stickle? We have Guzman, a warrant for your arrest. Questions for Moloch. My men are posted..."

Another screen, fedora filled. From his hand, a flash of orange, a popping crack. Karaki gone in splintered glass...

"Bruce is finished meal."

"Overseas. A.F. East. Bloodwurst here, Maddox. Screen Foreign One. Cost overruns, unions fighting installation of robettes. All in Shumley's Redbook. One second—Video Zero now printing: Petro kidnapped. Ransom of ten million. Need instructions to—"

"Eh, later Cranston, we have a situation—"

"Horace, this is Ethel. You cannot—this is not allowed...You can do better than..."

"You must listen to the woman, my good chap. Do her bidding. Right, Mother?"

"My dress, these stains. Awful..."

Listen? Maybe he should have listened to Ethel. Home was home, office another can of...And *better.* Well, who didn't

140

want to do, be, better?

"*Butter?* I tell vut *butter* iss, Stuckle. *Butter* iss more fucktries, fud, und—Dum mashin...Luk, spills...Whuckenburry spik of invisibil propurty in der head: privut property uff mind vurkers. Vee dunt allow dot. How vee force our pipples share zat, pruduce eet? Dot is maginashun, der fairy tells. I cunt, vont allow dis ting..."

The Premier, on his feet, waving a glass, advancing toward him—a molting bear, glasses glinting, piece of shrimp dangling from his beard.

"Move back, Mr. Premier. Please, no further." His voice, strangled, a far-off cry. Crazy, they must think him...Whatever he'd say...useless...The Premier back in his chair, glaring, gulping wine.

"Bruce needs instructions."

"*Bloodwurst signing off. To the Cliffhags. Vacation time, old boy. You must visit—*"

Another pop and Bloodwurst gone in shards of glass. Words, unbidden, rising quickly to his lips and lost.

And now again a host of faces rippling screens. More snaps and cracks with people diving for the floor. Not to hurt, oh no not that: just the faces, make them vanish into night. There and there and over *there,* Karaki sliding, gliding by, a smoking finger sighting him, while Mawsley following close behind kept blowing kisses, cheeks outpuffed. Now Ethel filled a screen, attacking air with slashing hands as Priddle—*Priddle?* —raised a middle finger, smiled. His mind, coconut—had it truly rebelled? Perhaps his eyes...Whatever he'd wanted to say—goose egg, no punch in, no...The mail hadn't gotten through, he'd failed...

Yet hadn't his father once said, "If you couldn't change the facts, change your perspective."

And Christ, Himself, no less, hadn't He spoken about those who were last—the lost, the failures—being first? In that event, Horace Stickle was doubtless on a comet to the top: the glass wasn't empty, it was full of air—hot air, no doubt, but...

A shout from a screen high on the wall. Back of a head. Red hair flowing over a collar.

"Smokey on Bandits. Popscicles identified. Hostile. We are under attack. Silos one through...Can't decipher, repeat...circuits jammed, fuses...War

141

games over. Cancel three. Recording, recording..."

"Shumley here, Monitor Red. Standby. She be the gas or vapor on Floor Ten, Fourteen, Eighteen, Twenty-niner. Should get 'er on out. I repeat..."

"Dot iss ohdur rutten iggs, nyet?"

The Russian Premier polishing his glasses, huffing, scrubbing the lenses. God he was tired. The gun?: on the floor. So was he: face down on the rug—arms, body, pinned. Hands rifling his person, grunts, the bark of command. People surfacing from under the table. Monitors babbling.

"Whackenberry back. Hi ho. Murray is on its way up. Everything is fine. Really must run."

"...Shumley again, she be..."

"Doctor Foch speaking. The basement reservoirs are being sealed..."

"Want a meal, a meal, a?..."

"Luck, der ductor iss fightink vit der dug."

"Bone to monitors: This here is Ralph Bone..."

"Foch to Control: The dog apparently succumbed..."

"Iss der Burt dud?"

"Come to ole Ralpho, Bart. Heel 'er up...."

"Strange odor, Mr. Moloch. Should we leave?—"

"Yes, Mr. President. Time for the TV demonstration of our pilot project. Robotized customer service at...hmmm, Pig-Wig, our giant grocery—"

"Mrs. Ralpher, you wanted—"

"The floor, building, Mr. Moloch—quivering. Is it?..."

"Heh, tremors, Mrs. Ralpher, we get—Watch!...the cart... falling!..."

"Luk, Broosh is on der buck like Burt und—Mun at vindo! Fullink! *See!* Vee must—"

"That you on monitor, H.S.? Stinky here. I'd take 'em on down freight emergency. End of hall, exit Zero. Load 'er off in the caverns, Section Niner, Fiver. I repeat folks, follow Horseshit. Hah, I mean, Stickle. He knows—"

"Stinky, where?..." People running, stumbling. He was free, standing. Shumley exploding into fractured rainbows. Chaos on monitor: mushroom clouds, a rain of rubble. Gorshev at the window. Things—bodies, objects?—hurtling by. Ball of fire on the horizon? Chandelier swaying, falling, crashing onto Bruce—the contraption, a roach upended, pincers groping, snapping air. Now rolling on its side, rising.

"Bruce goes to freight. Return with food. Follow Bruce."

"Crowling here, Monitor Zero-Chips. Ivan alert. Ivan Ivan. This is not a recording. I repeat, Crowling here. The pops-cicles..."

"President Rulphur, I haff nut cummunded an attuck—"

"Where's the phone? For God's sake, Slannery, the Red!—"

"Ladies and gentlemen, I am Horace Stickle. Stinky—Mr. Shumley has told us—"

"Slannery, the bloody *phone,* man! Thank—the damn machine, it's grabbed, smashing..."

"Bruce feeds fine people to food. Goes freight."

"Follow me, please ladies and gentlemen. Shumley knows. It's down here!" Was it? Who could tell?

They were looking his way. The gun, forgotten, at least for now. His legs were numb, time-locked in neutral. Premier Gorshev was right: The smell of rotten eggs was in the air. And he didn't need an information revolution to tell him that.

14

HAD EVERYONE MANAGED to get on the elevator? Voice control had not worked to prevent Bruce from crowding itself in among the passengers. The President, jammed beside him, tugged at his collar, coughed hoarsely. Was he fifty or a hundred? Berry eyes glittered in the ivory face; hair, black, a pompadour that flowed in upward sweeps and curls, then plunged darkly to the neckline. Mouth puckered, purplish, with wrinkle sunbursts at the corners; forehead smooth, unlined, but now laced with sweat.

"Mr. President, this may be my last opportunity to say..." Metal gleaming, gun nuzzling his ribs. Iron grip on both arms. Ralpher speaking.

"Hate small places!...like a sardine! Bothers me terrible. I—"

"Bruce serves appetizers."

"Shut up, I say! Ridiculous damn—"

"Father, be quiet, we'll be down in no time, won't we Mr.?..."

"Stickle, Mrs. President—Ralpher. I'm sorry about...Yes, we're moving..." Wrists being bent, twisted. Handcuffs, were they trying to put?...

"Lost the phone, Mother. Cursed machine, cramming all of

us. I—up there, the screen by the ceiling. That man..."

"We interrupt regular programming for a brief newsbreak. This just in: All, and I repeat, all drug charges have been dropped against Flash Stud of Crud!"

"Unverified reports allege—we are experiencing interference—that some major oil installations, cities...nuclear skirmish...hit...Peace talks continue...major powers...Attention...an attempt..."

"Vut is der Crud to do vit zis whar, Mister Presdunt?"

"...on the life of the President..."

"What, Mr. Premier? Sorry. Detest people, swarms—breaks me out in the sweats, hives...Nothing important is it, Mr. Moloch?"

"More gaming, no doubt, Mr. President. A scenario for the military, brainstorming. Crowling is strong on that."

"Bruce has ice cream to put in fine people's bowels."

"...Detectives Karaki and Fasten advise—a Rickle, no Thurmond...believed dangerous...Indictments...Amalgamated...Moloch...papers seized...a Guzman..."

"This here is Shumley in the upper right of the freight 'mergency monitor. Youse is stopped till Bone gets the back-up goin'. I'se jus play up sum music on the audio whiles we's waitin', folks."

"EARL WRANGLER HERE WITH 'BALLIN' MY BABY'..."

"...Developments on the Crud case as they occur. Now back..."

"Good grief, the lights—"

"It's all right, Father, the screen is still lit. We can see—"

"Mr. President, would you please listen to me for a minute? There are millions of people who are losing...it's not just jobs, but themselves, the things they stand for, because of this revolution, and—" A hand clamped over his mouth.

"Where's Slannery? Don't we have another phone? Intolerable. Slannery, what the hell?—Mother, the pen flashlight, your purse..."

"Mr. President, with computers and robots taking..." Only a mumble, the hand on his mouth tightening. Ralpher not listening anyway. Staring at the screen. Silos opening, giant mouths, silver tongues thrusting skywards. A woman in tights, tap-dancers. Hands wrenching at the waistband of jockey shorts.

146

"Crowling back, Maddox. We've lost visual. This test needs revision. Guidance systems reversed trajectory on the Big Cigar after zero niner. Gatler has been contacted—"

"Vut gud is dot? Missul lund buck ver it vas lunched. Iss diss yur revlooshun? Everysing spidded up? More prublums?"

"*OH BALLIN' BONNY, AINT IT GRAND—YEAH, OH...*"

Dropping rapidly, a smashing jolt. Bell jangling, doors skidding open with a jarring bounce. Darkness. That whistling? —wind, insistent, pushing, tugging. Bruce clanking from the elevator into the gloom, pincers grabbing air, its rods moving in spastic semaphore.

"Mother! *Mother,* are you there! The flashlight..."

"*SHUMLEY ON CAVERN AUDIO AND MONITORS. BACK-UP'S GONE. BONE SAYS SHE LOST A WHEEL. YOUSE IS OFF SEWERLINE FIVE NEAR PIG-WIG PLAYLAND. WATER BE FLOODIN' THAT AREA SOON. TAKE 'ER STRAIGHT AHEAD, I REPEAT, 'ROUND THE BEND, UP AND OVER.*"

"Ladies and gentlemen, Maddox Moloch, speaking. Pig-Wig at Groine Street is our main—Good god!...*water*...is it?..."

"HALLOO! THIS IS CONTROLLER. WILL YOU PLEASE GET OUT OF TUNNEL OF WINDS! PIRATES' DEN IS THE OTHER WAY! GET BACK IN YOUR BOATS OR WE'LL NOTIFY SECURITY! I REPEAT..."

"Mother!"

"No, it's me, Mr. President, Horace Stickle. Let me help..."

Rafts drifting toward them. Was that gunfire, beyond the drawbridge ahead? Red lightning, howling, from caves pocketing the walls.

"Here, Mr. President, I have a boat. There, step—whoops..."

Sprawled in the bottom, but the President was aboard. That was the important thing. Now to just...

"Damn it, Slannery. *Slannery,* get your ass—"

"Father, I'm alright. You must keep your feet dry."

"Miz Rulphur is vit me, Mr. Presdunt. Vee go."

"You there! Get away from the President. Let me—God—dam..."

"*Slannery,* where?..."

"In the water, Mr. President. I can't swim. Oh lord, sinking!—"

"*SHUMLEY ON THE SPEAKERS. STINKY HERE, H.S.*

147

*TREMORS OR WHATEVER DONE LOOSED UP THE KENNELS.
THE LITTER BE RUNNIN' FREE. REPEAT, THEY'S OUT DOWN
CHUTE THREE."*

*"WHACKENBERRY, VIDEO TWO, CELLAR SYSTEM.
EXPLOSIONS HAVE AFFECTED HATCHERY EXITS SEVEN,
ELEVEN. BEWARE OF YELLOWHEADS. THEY MAY HAVE
ROTATED SPAR CHIPS..."*

"YO HO HO, I'M CAPTAIN CRUD. GRIND YOUR BONES..."

"You there! What in blazes?—"

"Horace Stickle's the name, Mr. President, and—Your
hand, away from the water!—*up!*"

Jaws opening, rows of teeth. Alligator!—toy? A swirl of
water, shadows moving on the wall. Candles flickering in
crevices, water dripping overhead. Ahead, stairs...Something
coming around the bend, splashing. A man, something else?:
lines of creatures, two legs, three?—tails? Lights blinking,
yellow dots from chest to head.

"Slannery, for Jesus sake, where!...Prinkle, you must!—"

"We'll get out here, Mr. President! Those stairs, that ramp!
Hurry!"

Another raft pulling alongside. Arms reaching for the
President. Rifles, pistols—pointing at him? A violent shove,
floating away, the creatures closer. A ladder on the wall to his
right. Paddle with his hands. Almost...there, he had a rung.
Something grabbing his leg—kick. Now at his coat, ripping,
torn away. Free. Up quickly. Another level. Concrete tunnel,
gloomy. Small gauge railroad tracks. A blast of whistle,
rumbling wheels, then a headlight round the bend. To his left,
a door, then stairs. Light ahead, yes sky, that violet twilight
arched above. But it was only afternoon. So quiet too, a silent
hum that filled his head.

Piles of rubble treetop high. And here and there a tangled
shape and crimson stain. Someone emerging from the subway
exit across the street. Good, not alone...Damn, winking
yellow...Must move away. There, in front, a half a block,
could it be?—the A.F. Pig-Wig standing firm. Yet towering,
circling, round the store, piles of concrete strewn through
with—mannequins?—crumpled things that didn't move. And
far beyond, behind the waste, were flashings, lightnings,
yellowish orange, that trembled through the skyline fires.

The store, hushed, empty. "Anybody here! I say, is?..."

A crash from outside: the Pig-Wig sign—the *Pig* portion leaning crookedly against the window. Movement, the floor shifting as if on rollers. Bottles falling, smashing glass; now music wafting overhead.

> *"Sigh-AYE-lunt night, Oh-ILY-night,*
> *Ahhl is cahm, ahll iss brite."*

A recording, choir. Voices, crystal slivers in his brain. Dizzy, waves of nausea. Up the aisle, a figure, silhouette, moving his way slowly? Stocky, outline blurred. The person sweeping goods from shelves, bashing into cans pyramided high on display. Eyes filming, objects spinning slowly into mists that coiled and swirled. Rippling lights, a blow, then falling as a voice came faintly from above.

"...Wench will replace food stuffs and dispense goods for customer. We aim to please."

The creature reaching down to pick him up, then hoist him high atop a stack of cans that quivered, swayed.

A groaning crack, a pistol shot that knifed the floor in jagged lines. Explosive snappings overhead.

> *"Round yon vir-HER-gin, mu-THER and child..."*

For a moment he felt peaceful, even joyous. King of the castle, he was, Monarch of Pig-Wig. By the front of the store, those things on dollys, red lights glowing: cameras?—TV? Hadn't Moloch at the office mentioned a demonstration, the pilot project?...Over there, and *there* too: screens—TVs alright. That was him, wasn't it?—lit up in brilliant color?: H.S., himself, being beamed across the land: a Ruler about to address his kingdom.

Something wrong, though, about that idea. People, were there any left to?...The parking lot, something moving, lines of forms, shadows...The voice again.

"I am Wench. What do you want?"

The creature right below him now, lights rippling, winking. A sudden hum, then two red orbs, bulbous eyes that tilted up, head rotating side-to-side. Strange, it seemed natural to answer the creature.

"Want?—me? Hard to say. It's more what I can't get back. Know what I mean?" Skull numb, a burning flash across his chest.

149

"Customer tell Wench. What do you want?"

Now, when it didn't matter—like' always—the words were coming, blooming before him, at his tongue.

"I want answers, since you ask, Wench. Answers. What good is all this information?—these technologies...the Revolution people are talking about—if we forget how to feel, care, be kind; if life becomes a huge computer game, a...a frenzied rush to dim arcades and pulsing lights? If we see ourselves as little more than programs flickering in the night. Answers?: There's too many and too few. Either way, I feel shut out. Pylor was right, I didn't get my equations straight, ended up pushing carts—empty ones."

Strange, not hot anymore. Cold, a chill climbing his limbs. Vision clearing, clouding, fractured as through splintered glass. Color fading, movement stopped: an ancient film in black and white—a frozen frame that...Faces, masks, at storefront windows. The swish and chunk of sliding doors, while shapes flowed through to fill the aisles. Was that his voice?

"...So Wench, it's a war of kinds, I guess, a fight to get on, survive oneself, the System—whatever that is—stake new claims, forge new worlds. Perhaps be better than I ever thought I could be. But the times...perhaps I don't belong, fit..."

"Wendy help Consumer."

"Thank you." The chill was gone, dissolving into burning cold, a spasmed ache behind his eyes.

"Wendy like customer."

His words freestyling again, coming from a vast distance, ticking faintly far beyond him. *Like?* Well that's okay, I guess. But you know, Wench, just for once, I'd rather matter, really matter, to someone, to a cause, to something out there... beyond, larger than what I am, something I truly care about, that cares about me too. Maybe just once be a hero, even to myself, if only for a moment...Silly, I guess, dreaming dreams, having expectations, ideas that leap reason and touch the stars. But to lose hope, Wench, fail to keep the faith in anything, is sort of like losing what I am down deep—is to become... well, a mouse that nibbles life away, a thing forever grey and dead, destroyed by tremors, silent bombs inside myself. That's an evil too, don't you think, Wench? Something bad that..."

Forgotten what he was going to say. Wench nodding and shaking her head. He felt a strange closeness toward the

150

creature. Talking *with* somebody for once, saying things he felt. But Wench wasn't a somebody, *he* was a somebody. He could cry and laugh, even think and reason with feeling. Perhaps man might someday be able to build life into beings far superior to himself in brainpower and physical ability. But would these newcomers really walk in their creator's footsteps, feel like him, reach his heights and touch his depths, possess his doubts? For that was part of the Word too, wasn't it?— that it carry heart, beat with the good in contention with the bad and unknown, the best that we feel and know, in our struggle with the worst, our greatest fears. It seemed so vital to believe that this was somehow true,that no matter what, he was more than Pylor's Xs and Ys, more than just a man (or woman, for that matter), trust that he—everyone—was something special, a human being, a special human being, perhaps in part only a steppingstone to a different, maybe higher form of being, but for now—always?—special, so very...

Overhead, a snapshot crack, a scream of steel. Then sky, a purpling scar, was arced above.

"Wench want cans. Customer move."

Wench, store, all fading into streaming dusk through which footsteps' clomp and creak were drawing near. A streak of grey—an arm, a hand?—reaching upward, toward him, far too close.

It had his leg, a shoulder wrenched. Behind him, good,an empy aisle. Yes, all clear to jump and run...*Run.* Who had said something about *not running* the other day?—or was it the other way round? *See how they run, see how...mattering, evil...*Words words words. But not the Word, a signature to light the dark, or at worst to hold it fast.

Thunderclap and storefront gone in clouds of dirt and gusting wind. A creature gripping ankle, knee, then moving on to leave him teetering and faint.

Something left to say—out there, circling, at his fingertips, almost touching, brushing past...

The veils descending, darkness close, with whipcrack, grinding, everywhere. And rising in the spreading gloom, a spiderweb of girder, beam, that hung suspended half a blink, then toppled through the swirling smoke. Now rain, a thousand pins against his face as metal talons raked his back. Almost

151

over, almost...Was that a cry or whistling wind? There, again, a feeble wail. An object, package, moving upwards toward him...

"Wench serves customer fine produce."

The cry again, a tiny sound. Reaching...in his arms...a child, a babe?...Rolling thunder, cannonades that boomed and tossed him to the heaving floor...

The bundle, gone. And by his side a crevass black and jagged stretched beyond his sight in yellow glare laced through with smoke. There, on the chasm's other lip, all blurred, a tiny hand, unblinking eyes so huge and...At last someone to save, give help, he must...

Leg's pinned...he had to reach across...stretch further, more...damn, slipping...grasp the fingers, arm, and pull...An empty socket, plastic arm—a Piggy Doll! It *talked*, it *peed*, it... Now his torso sliding, dangling down the crack...Then plunging into sulphured dark to cut the cold and endless space until...

For just a moment he escaped and hovered in a shaft of light that lit the wasteland far below where yawning fissures crisscrossed earth and swallowed up the metal creatures battling there. And deep in Pig-Wig's rubble, all alone, a robot—Wench? —still piling cans that tumbled down. Then on the wind from far away the voices came...

"Slee-eep in heav-enly pea-eece, sleep...
Fa la la la la la la la la.
Merry Christmas from Brew..."

...before the blackness closed again. And from the rushing dark that swept him on, more murmurs, echoes, whispered past.

"Deduction Stickle, no punch out, no...
We must be men, not mice, not...
A coward who doesn't run...
One, good, clean memory...
H.S. that you? Youse not lost now, not lost at all, at all, at all, at..."

Shumley was wrong, though, this time. He was lost alright: the night a blackened claw that hurled him down and down. But it didn't matter, not at all. Because for once he was going flat out, into the darkness, charged with a fierce joy that would not be denied, with the knowledge that like a dubious Kilroy, he had been there, tried, was still there as long as he burned, until the flame went out...

152

About the Author

DOUGLAS H. YOUNG is a Canadian born on April Fools' Day, 1938. An attorney, he received his first law degree from Osgoode Hall Law School of York University in Toronto, Canada. He holds, as well, Master of Laws degrees in International Law and Investment from both New York and Harvard Universities and has been an executive of Celanese and Exxon Corporations in Manhattan as well as of Creole Petroleum, Exxon's previously owned affiliate in Caracas, Venezuela. Mr. Young has also been an Assistant Professor of Law and International Affairs at Carleton University in Ottawa, Canada. He now lives in Fort Lauderdale with his wife and daughter where he is engaged in private law practice and is presently at work on another novel.